'A model wife' and other tales:

A collection of short stories

Sally Nicol

CONTENTS

ACKNOWLEDGEMENTS

With special thanks to my sister in law Karen for her feedback and encouragement as I have developed my writing and story-telling skills.

Also, to my friend Jane for her championing of my efforts.

Thanks to Harvie for helping me to navigate putting this book together.

FORWARD

I love words. A well-constructed sentence gives me visceral pleasure. When reading, if a phrase pleases me, I will roll it around my tongue, prolonging the delight, admiring its lightness, re-reading it over and over to drink every drop from it. For some, it will be standing before a beautiful painting, or listening to a haunting piece of music, both of which I enjoy and admire, but a clever description or observation will sing out from a page for me and it is this which gives me perhaps the greatest satisfaction of all.

I have always been an avid reader and was gifted as a teenager with excellent teachers who instilled within me a deep appreciation of words. I learned to value the glorious complexity of the English language, and as I grew older I increasingly found that I did my best thinking with a pen in my hand. Thoughts I did not even know existed would appear on the paper in front of me, allowing me to have a sort of conversation with myself. My own character can emerge on the page, sometimes surprising me. My pen has captured moments of confusion and exhilaration, disappointment and gratitude. In our early marriage, my husband was the surprised recipient of occasional letters in which I would pour out my thoughts and feelings when I was only in the next room or even the same room as him! I wrote copious letters to friends in my late teens and early twenties, as well as keeping diaries containing all my thoughts and experiences; in my thirties and forties this morphed into keeping journals as I charted my life and my spiritual journey, as well as dabbling in a bit of poetry writing; and now in my fifties, I have begun exploring creative writing, sometimes revisiting experiences from my life, incorporating characters that I have encountered into my work or losing myself in my imagination as I attempt to create a story.

When reading, I enjoy a good plot but mostly I love a well-drawn character such as Count Fosco in Wilkie Collins's "The woman in white" - larger than life, dangerous and evil yet with charm and comedy, or Count Alexander Rostov in Amor Towles's "A gentleman in Moscow" - wise and witty, beautifully brought to life through a mastery with words. Of course, one of the great masters of describing a character to perfection was Charles Dickens.

I have discovered that my writing leans more to character than to plot as I enjoy developing personality and temperament, trying to see the world through the eyes of my cast, trying to understand their psychology and how they might react in a given situation. If I meet an interesting person or notice something about somebody, I will try to capture them in words on paper or on my mobile. I will store these descriptions and turn to them for inspiration when forming a story.

Last year, while resting on a bench in the sunshine while my husband was taking some photographs, a breeze began to rustle through the trees, and the way that it travelled around the semi-circle of trees almost made them look like they were doing a Mexican wave! I immediately took out my phone to make a note of what had happened, for use in a future story. A number of years ago, after completing a painting course, I found that I began looking at the world through colour, looking around me and deciding which hue would best describe it on paper. Nowadays I am painting word pictures all the time.

I have a little granddaughter of three and I love to note down the amusing things she does, the observations she makes, and even the way she skips ahead of us. These things find their way into my stories and I feel as if I have captured her forever and can enjoy those pleasures again and again. Such is the joy of writing!

My husband has grown used to me disappearing into my study (a converted bedroom) mid-way through putting away the laundry or cleaning the bathroom as an idea strikes me which I want to capture. I can lose all sense of time as an hour turns into four hours before I stand from my desk with aching hips.

I do not always like to end a story with everything sewn up and explained, preferring to leave things open-ended for the reader to draw their own conclusions. After all, in book clubs, our discussions are usually more interesting if people can explore how they feel the story has ended! I would love to think that a reader will find something of worth to discuss about a character that I have conceived. In writing his fairy tales, Hans Christian Anderson would use this technique to great effect, and are not all stories birthed from the fairy tale genre, when people would pass on their tales to the next generation in the oral tradition before stories were set down on paper? Life is usually not neat – indeed it can often be messy and unpredictable, and so, sometimes, we can allow our stories to reflect that.

Writing short stories is a reward in itself, even if the story is never read by anybody outside of the family. Sitting quietly, developing the characters, and choosing the correct words can be stimulating and exciting, and, just occasionally, I will look at a sentence I have written and be thrilled with the impact of the words on the page, let them roll around my mouth, let them shape my lips and ingest their   delight.

A MODEL WIFE

Patricia MacArthur guessed that something was wrong as soon as she heard Michael's voice. His voice thundered and roared, heavy and powerful enough to cause small vibrations in the floorboards. Even when not angered Michael's voice could sound like the rumble of a train passing through an underground station, or when heard from another room as if a cushion had been placed over his face but his voice had somehow managed to escape. Right now though, he was angry, and Patricia suspected that she knew why. She had been exposed. Her secret was hidden no more and she was to suffer the consequences. Perhaps it was for the best. A secret is a heavy burden to carry, and its weight increases the longer it is held. But how had her clandestine activities been uncovered? Who had revealed her, condemning her to a choice which would test her resolution once and for all? And what would be Michael's reaction?

Not that Michael was a cruel man – no, she could never accuse him of that - and he had never pretended to be anything but himself; it was she that had not been completely honest with him.

Patricia had been raised by parents who had married later in life and were, therefore older than many of her friends' parents. They were old-fashioned in their outlook on life and their expectations. Mother had remained at home to care for Patricia and her brother Edward while their father worked long hours to support the family. Patricia was expected to play the part of a dutiful daughter, helping in the home and learning those essential skills of a homemaker such as sewing, baking, and perhaps a little gardening. Ambition had been discouraged, being considered irrelevant. While many of her friends had worked their way through a series of boyfriends, she had lived a relatively sheltered life in the suburbs, away from many of the temptations of the city. She had completed her education at school to 'A' 'levels but hadn't any real plans of what to do with her life, so had drifted into a job in a large dental practice, working on the reception desk.

She met Michael on her first day when he came into the reception area to enquire after the notes of his patient. He was wearing a face mask and so she had only a limited impression of him – his head was heavy and round, with dark brows which formed a tick over each eye, declaring them present and correct. His eyes were brown, attentive, and focused on the job in hand. He hadn't seemed to notice that she was new and a little nervous, such was his intensity in his quest, and she had felt intimidated by him. Over time she became impressed by his authority, his absolute certainty in whatever he did, and when he finally did notice her and ask her to join him for a meal, she happily succumbed. Her parents were equally dazzled by his brilliance and very soon she found herself engaged to be married. He enjoyed her eagerness to please, her submission, even subservience, to his authority, and it appeared to all to be a perfect match. Patricia did have some misgivings and lying alone in bed at night she would even go so far as to say that they were most definitely mismatched, but she hadn't the courage to say this 'out loud' in the daylight hours, for she alone knew that what the world saw was not the 'real her'. In her mind, alone in the dark, she was not Patricia but Patty; not a person creeping about those around her, afraid to challenge the status quo or cause trouble but a free spirit, reacting spontaneously to events without planning or preparation. As 'Patty' she was no longer be invisible – people would notice her immediately, be drawn to her as a bee is to pollen. Happiness is a cheerful yellow sunflower displaying all its glorious colour as it turns its face to the sun, and this was the real Patty, but only when she was alone, and only when the sun had gone down. It was a mirage, an illusion, because Patricia was expected to fit neatly into her place and cause as little disruption to her family as possible. It was a simple as that. And for twenty years that was the role she had played. She had delivered two healthy boys to Michael, stayed at home to look after them as her mother had done before her, and submitted any ambition or dreams at the altar of her family, but this had all changed 6 months ago.

Since their youngest son had left home to go to university Patty had suddenly found that she had more hours in the day than she had ever had before. Michael, now running his own private practice and working very long hours, was often not home before 8 o'clock in the evenings, sometimes even later. Patty would have her chores finished by 2.30 pm and would not be required to prepare the evening meal for some time, so she had begun to spend more time dawdling in the town centre. It was here that she first spotted the poster advertising life drawing classes – *'no experience required, beginners welcome'.* She had photographed the leaflet on her phone and had frequently glanced at the advert, a little shiver of excitement running through her body each time she furtively did so. Could she? What would Michael say? Would he approve? She felt sure that he would not approve – his old-fashioned approach to life had, if anything, become even more entrenched. He would be horrified to think of her staring at the naked body of a stranger, in public. But would he ever need to know? Some of the sessions were in the late afternoon or early evening and finished well before Michael returned home. After a couple of weeks deliberating, with some trepidation and excitement in equal measure, she signed up for the class.

On entering the studio, (actually a rented room in the local council offices), Patty's senses were struck powerfully by the smells of paint, turps, charcoal, and fresh paper; easels were arranged in a circle around two staging blocks, and a few people were setting up, preparing their materials, papers, and canvases for the forthcoming challenge. Patty assessed her fellow students. A young, dark-haired girl sat to her left, hair tied back in a pony-tail, which already supported a couple of brushes roughly threaded through, giving an aura of being an experienced participant of the class. Patty wondered at her age – if nudity was involved, would people be expected to present their identification to prove their age? She blushed to think of her inexperience at the age of this young girl. Next to the girl was a woman of around 40, not dissimilar in age to Patty herself, who was planning to use charcoal on a huge sheet of paper. She was arranging sticks of charcoal of varying thicknesses on a small table next to her, some of which looked so fragile that she wondered they didn't just disintegrate as soon as a person held them in their hands; she smiled at Patty when she glanced up and saw her watching.

"First time?" she asked.

Patty nodded, relieved that somebody had noticed her. "I'm a bit nervous. I've never done anything like this before"

"Don't worry," said the girl with the pony-tail, "We all have to start somewhere. Just ask if you need any help, we're a friendly gang here."

"That we are," smiled a grey-haired old gentleman on the opposite side of the room, who had set out an array of coloured pencils beside him.

By the time the class was ready to begin Patty was beginning to feel more relaxed and looking forward to the experience. She had treated herself to a tin of pencils ranging from soft to hard, and a good eraser for what she imagined would be many mistakes. She had opted for one of the smaller pads of drawing paper, intimidated by the prospect of having to fill a large area.

The model was an elderly man who entered wearing a white towelling dressing gown. The teacher instructed him quietly about what she wanted from him and then turned to the class.

"Martin is going to maintain each position for three minutes before moving on to the next. Don't worry if you haven't completed your work. This is about capturing the essence of movement. It's about large sweeping arcs with your materials. I don't want any of you getting too bogged down with detail. You won't have time. Each time he changes position turn your page, or go to another part of your canvas and begin the new sketch. There will be 5 positions and then we will let Martin take a break".

With that, she turned and smiled at Martin, who discarded his dressing gown and adopted the first pose. Patty was astonished at the ease with which he exposed his body to strangers. Naked as the day he was born, he stood with legs astride, torso slightly turned to his left and one arm outstretched as if pointing to something in the distance. His flesh was saggy and lined, the muscle falling away from bone. There was a suggestion of tan lines on some parts of his body and his face was resting as if his mind was elsewhere, beyond the limits of the room. Patsy soon found that she was so absorbed in trying to capture the suggestion of the lines of the body that she forgot she was looking at a naked man. Her embarrassment gone, she began to enjoy the experience. She could hardly believe it when he put his gown back on and it was time for a break. She had the opportunity to admire the work of her fellow students whilst enjoying a cup of tea and a biscuit and then they regrouped for the second session. She had floated home that evening, feeling exhilarated with her new experience. Before Michael had returned home she had arranged her work on the double bed to assess her achievements. They weren't terrible, though she did have some room for improvement.

Her confidence grew with each class and she was building up quite a portfolio – she had progressed onto charcoal drawings with the encouragement of her new friends, but she hadn't yet plucked up the courage to try other mediums. Some weeks they had concentrated on portraits, zooming in on the faces of a variety of models and she learned to appreciate the character and experience brought to a face which had wrinkles and blemishes. She found that as she carried out the weekly shopping she was paying more attention to the faces of those she encountered, imagining how she would translate their features in charcoal and pencil. Martin had returned to the class a few times and she had gathered the courage to speak with him about how it felt to be a life drawing model. She was intrigued to know where he went mentally when he was posing – did he meditate? Did it take a lot of concentration to hold the pose? Did he have no inhibitions at all about being naked in front of strangers? Martin had explained that he had never felt so free as when he stood atop those staging blocks. He felt no responsibility to live up to anybody's expectations. This was him, exactly as he was. Unmasked. No pretense. Over the following weeks Patty spoke with some of the female models too and they expressed that same sense of freedom. The body shapes of the women varied hugely, few of them embodying the so-called perfect form suggested by the media. She saw skin dimpled with cellulite and broken veins, skin that threatened to tear as it stretched over bony protuberances; skin marked by stretch marks; large breasts, sagging breasts, and breasts that had barely begun to grow. Rather than causing the group to make judgements, all of these bodies were celebrated for their intriguing shapes, sharp edges and curves. Each one was different, fascinating, and honoured. Six weeks ago, Patty had approached the teacher and asked for an opportunity to pose herself.

She could hardly believe that she had done it! Driving home that evening she had been tempted to telephone and explain that she had changed her mind, but Michael had returned from work, tired and distracted, and she had once again spent an evening in his company feeling invisible. Having lived a lifetime of submitting to the expectations of others she had decided on that evening that this was her moment. Michael would never understand. He considered art to be a form of pornography and often scoffed at sculptures and paintings of nudes, wondering how 'the perverts got away with it'. This would be her secret and he need never know. Patty yearned to be known, really known, not for who people thought she was, but who she really was. Not the docile Patricia but the free spirit Patty.

She had enjoyed the experience so much that she had now posed several times for the group. She felt their intense examination of her body as their pencils and paintbrushes created replicas of her form. She exhilarated in feeling their eyes taking in her stretch marks which spoke of life borne into the world; she relished their examination of her breasts, no longer as pert as they once were, but speaking of her womanhood; she appreciated their examination of her most secret places as an unravelling of the mystery of Patty MacArthur, recently delivered into the world of light after many years being hidden in the dark. And now it seemed her secret had been disclosed and there would be a reckoning.

The ticking of the clock seemed to be baiting her, counting down the minutes and seconds while she vacillated on the stairs. As the large hand on the clock made its way steadily to 12 it threatened to expose her, to shout out "Here she is. She's here!" In the half-light the mahogany body of the clock, standing about 6 feet tall, resembled a thin man hiding in the shadows, limbs held in close lest he be seen. She was fixed to the spot, her feet immovable as if cement was hardening around them. She drew in a deep breath, brought her shoulders up tall and prepared to stride into the room, ready to stand her ground, no longer prepared to be invisible but to be noticed, to be celebrated and loved.

A PRIVATE SORROW

I am wide awake! It's gone 1 am and I have been awake for 19 hours, yet my mind remains alert and my body restless. Sleep seems as elusive as a Bittern in the reedbed. I glance across at Betty, still asleep with her hair in curlers, her mouth slightly open and her breathing steady. Steady is a word that sums Betty up perfectly – stable, balanced, unchanging. She's been a good wife these past 60 years and we've been content enough, drifting through family life with few arguments and barely a raised voice. She's been a wonderful mother to our three boys and they have never wanted for attention or care. Leaving the bed as quietly as this creaky old body will allow me, I make my way to the kitchen to put the kettle on, surrendering to insomnia.

Waiting for the water to boil I take a seat on the chair, shaking my head at the ludicrous need to rest when I have just left my bed because I couldn't sleep. Inside I still feel like a young man, ready to take on the world, ready to charge out like an unbroken horse in a rodeo, faster than a sprinter off the starting blocks. But my body is wrecked by arthritis, legs weak, joints sore, walking with a rocking gait like a boat being pitched by the waves, each step carefully placed in case I am knocked off balance abruptly. I lift the kettle and begin to pour the water into the mug, my hand shaking with the weight and causing me to spill some of the water onto the worktop. I place the mug on my kitchen trolley and walk through with it to my riser-recliner chair, where I will probably spend the rest of the night. Tomorrow, or should I say later today, I am visiting the Imperial War Museum at Salford Docks with the U3A, and I'm looking forward to returning to my old stomping ground, the first time in a little under sixty years. I put the radio on quietly as I drink my tea and Buddy Holly is singing "Peggy Sue"; I close my eyes and I can see her, a faint flush in her cheeks as her friends say "He's singing to you!" and drag her onto her feet. *"Peggy Sue, Peggy Sue, oh how my heart yearns for you, oh Peggy, my Peggy Sue......."*

*

The minibus arrives promptly at 10.15 and Bill, one of our younger members at only 60 years old, is today's nominated driver. There are a few of the younger boys who take turns on our trips out, helping out with the old fogies with lots of ribbing and good humour. They're good lads and I don't know what we'd do without them. I'd be trapped in that flat all the time and I honestly think I'd do myself in one of these days. The trips out once a month are a lifeline to me, and I think Betty's grateful for them too, to get me out from under her feet. Bill brings out the wheelchair and pushes it to my door. I step hesitantly over the threshold, taking care not to catch my toes. Flying out nose first and hitting the ground with a thump is not the way I prefer to say hello to the lads! I hand my sticks to Bill and allow him to propel me to the rear of the bus, where he presses the button for the electric lift to lower for the wheelchair. Before long the chair is strapped to the floor and we're on our way, a low rumble of voices filling the confined space as the boys share their stories of National Service or previous visits to the War Museum. I allow the noise to drift over me as my own memories begin to flood back, playing in my head like an old VHS recording, sometimes the picture being grainy and indistinct, other times crystal clear.

I was sixteen when I began my apprenticeship as an engineer at Trafford Park. I can remember arriving by bus from my home in Salford, looking around me with an open mouth. I could see green fields stretching out, I felt like I was in the countryside. And cows! Where I lived, it was just street after street of terraced housing, no gardens, and very little sky. My Dad was so chuffed that I had got this apprenticeship – "It'll give you opportunities I never 'ad, son. Make sure you make the best of it. Keep yer head down, get on with yer work, and you might even end up in one of them nice houses they've got down there when you get married." Get married! I was only 16 and a half, but Mam and Dad had already decided that me and Betty would make a good match, Betty being the 16-year-old daughter of one of Dad's work pals. And Betty was alright, she was pretty and sweet and no bother. I was happy enough taking her for a walk or to the pictures.

Getting off the bus that first day, I joined the snake of people making their way to the factories, thousands of them! I remember seeing one lad on his bike and the crowds were so big he didn't even pedal as he was swept along with them. The factories had been making the engines for the Lancaster Bombers and Spitfires in the war, and although not at the height of its production anymore, there were still about 50, 000 people working there, and now I was one of them. I felt proud as a peacock and was keen to make my Mam and Dad proud.

Bill parks the minibus up and comes to the rear to undo the straps that hold the wheelchair in place. "Last in, first out eh, John?"

"Aye, lad," I say. "Cheers mate"

While everybody else makes their way off the bus I look around me. The canals are still here, but that's about all that remains of those times. The old factories were pulled down, as well as the housing that had seemed so fancy to me then, with their little three-foot gardens and fancy-sounding street names like in New York , 1st Street, 5th Street. The War Museum itself is a huge, impressive structure made of three interlocking sections that's supposed to represent earth, air, and water. The metal is gleaming in the bright sunshine and lifting my eyes to the top of the building makes me feel a bit dizzy.

When everybody is off the bus Bill leads the way, his role as designated driver extending to tour operator and guide! As Bill is pushing my wheelchair, I am the first to enter the building and I take in the open space of the foyer. It strikes me that the open space 'in my day' was in the distance and most definitely not within the buildings themselves, which were full of bodies milling around like ants. We make our way into the exhibition area and begin to look at the various archived objects depicting conflict, not only from the two world wars but even the modern-day war against terrorism. Being in a wheelchair can be a nuisance in some museums but here it works fine. I can see most of the displays but it's not really the war memorabilia that I'm here for. I want to step back into the past and remember. I decide to opt out of watching the film show and ask Bill to deposit me in the small café with a cup of tea.

As I drink my tea I hear the voice of Buddy Holly drifting over again from the radio playing behind the counter, singing *"Oh Peggy, my Peggy Sue, oh well I love you gal and I need my Peggy Sue"*.

"Are you alright, Sir?"

I blink and look at the young girl standing over me, concern showing in her eyes, and I realise that tears have wet my face.

"Aye, I'm fine love. Sorry. Just remembering."

"Are they happy tears or sad tears?", the lass says, taking a seat beside me. "It's not very busy here today. If you want to talk, I'm happy to listen."

"I was thinking about Peggy."

"Is that your wife?

"No, but maybe she could have been, if I was braver, stronger, more of a man."

The lass remained quiet.

"I was just a young lad, 16, with my whole life ahead of me. I had been given an opportunity. A chance my own Dad would have given his right arm for. An apprenticeship and a possibility, if I played my cards right, of a nice house right here in Trafford Park. They had my life all mapped out for me you see, Mam and Dad. We didn't really have teenagers in those days, you know. All the young lads just dressed like their dads! And there were rules to be followed. It wasn't unusual for families to have expectations of who you'd marry. You'd go steady for a bit, and then get married. I married Betty when I wasn't quite 19, but we'd been going steady since before I started my apprenticeship. Our dads were friends.

In my first week here I was invited to a party by one of the lads who lived in one of the fancy houses. It was on a Sunday afternoon and a few of the houses were getting together, a bit of a street party, you know. I turned up with my hair full of Brylcreem and my 'Sunday best' clothes and Alan met me off the bus. When we got to 5th Street it was all happening! Someone had the wireless on and music was playing, kids were out playing hopscotch and skipping and people were sitting around with their drinks. As soon as we turned the corner I saw this girl - she was beautiful. Blonde hair, curled and soft, I thought she looked the image of Ingrid Bergman. She had a gorgeous smile and was laughing with some other girls. She was wearing shorts and her legs were shapely, her waist tiny. She was perfection. Alan grinned as he watched me and said loudly, "Let me introduce you to my sister, Peggy Patterson. Peggy, this is John Wright, he works with me."

Peggy turned her face to me and I swear the sun was shining directly from that face. Her skin was as pretty and delicate as the flowers on a Cherry Blossom and I think I loved her from that moment. We spent the afternoon as a group together but all I can remember is Peggy. I can't remember who else was there, or what we said or did, I just remember her face. That Sunday was followed by other Sundays and we hung around together as a group. Sometimes we would go for a walk in the fields, chasing each other and breathing in all that fresh air. Sometimes we would take a picnic. Occasionally we'd go to the pictures to watch a film and Peggy and I always seemed to end up sitting next to each other. Once we went dancing and I held her in my arms, smelling the sweet perfume in her hair. My Mam and dad would sometimes ask why I wasn't meeting up with Betty and I would come up with some excuse or other. Sometimes Alan would seem to usher the others a bit of a distance away from me and Peggy. I think maybe he was giving us a bit of space. In those days it was up to the man to ask the lady for a date, but I couldn't bring myself to do that to Betty, or to disappoint Mam and Dad. Eventually, Peggy started to sit next to one of the other lads instead of me, and by the time I was 18, I was engaged to Betty and had stopped meeting up with them all on a Sunday.

We got married in 1960 and at our wedding party, the song "Peggy Sue" was played. I was dancing with Betty when it came on and she saw a change come over me but didn't know why. I brushed it off and pulled her into my arms, but that song was immediately followed by *"Who's sorry now"* by Connie Francis, *"Who's heart is achin' to breakin' each vow? Who's sad and blue, who's cryin' too? ….."* My hands were trembling and I felt sick. I had to run to the lav. It put a bit of a dampener on the rest of the proceedings, I can tell you. Betty was upset 'cause she felt like I just opted out of the rest of the party and I couldn't help wondering if I'd made the biggest mistake of my life.

And today, that's the second time I've heard Peggy Sue being played on the radio. Poor old Betty's at home, cleaning my house and looking after me and this silly old sod can't stop thinking about a girl from 60 years ago."

I can't talk anymore, the tears have started again. The young lass reaches forward to hold my shaking hand.

"It sounds to me like you've been a good husband to Betty for 60 years. Don't be too hard on yourself. Peggy's in your mind because of coming here and revisiting those old memories. Once you get back home and on with your normal life she'll probably go back to being a faded memory again."

I nod my head and pat her hand as she stands to return to her work. I take out a small black and white photograph from my wallet. Bringing it to my lips I kiss it and then return it to its private location, slip the wallet into my trousers and start to pull myself together before the boys join me for a cuppa.

SMELLING OF ROSES

The stale smell from the old rug made me feel so ashamed the last time I called the doctor. As she entered the door I could see the physical reaction, though she tried to cover it the best she could, 'forgetting' to close the door behind her so some fresh air could come into the room. I swore to myself at that moment that I would not be calling anyone else to my home, whether I feel unwell or not. I may have lost my mobility and my dignity but I have not lost my pride. Not yet, and nor do I ever intend to.

I've always kept a clean house, all my life. You could have eaten your dinner off the top of my sideboard, or off the floor. I would do the whole house, top and bottom, every couple of days. There were never stacks of laundry, dirty or clean, hanging around my house, though I suppose I didn't have multiple bodies to be looking after, it just being me and Harold.

I can remember when we first moved into this place – 'Rose Cottage'. Harold had said it had our name written all over it (well, mine anyway!) and it would be a perfect place for our little family, when it was time. When he had walked me along the Lane, he had stopped outside this beautiful cottage, with a small front garden bursting with roses of every colour. The fragrance of the roses was intoxicating, and the colours were a real treat for the eyes. A small, wrought iron gate led onto a winding path that was almost hidden by the lush blooms, and at the end was a wooden door painted cornflower blue. Harold went on to take such pride in those roses, but he would take me in his arms when he came in from the garden and remind me that I was the most precious Rose of all, his prize Rose. Now the garden is overgrown, given over to nature completely. Once Harold died there was nobody to look after it. My health had already been on the wane and the family we had hoped for never came.

And now, here I am, alone. Nobody to call on even if I wanted to. Which I don't, by the way. I am sitting here in my sofa chair, overflowing the space, my soft flesh finding its way into every corner like heated glue. My two huge, thick legs are resting on a low footstool, the skin scaly and flaking. My arms are flabby and the tissue under my upper arms sways back and forth whenever I move them. I can't lift my legs from the stool. They are too heavy. I've been stuck here in this chair now for three days. My clothes and the chair are wet because my bladder has opened several times. My bowels haven't opened yet but I am waiting for that inevitable, final indignity. If the Doctor had struggled to stop herself retching from the lack of air the last time, I dread to think what she would do this time. So, here I am. I suppose this is how it will end. One day somebody will come into the house and have to cover their nose and mouth at the stale, disgusting stench that will greet them, but I won't need to suffer the shame and the embarrassment because I will be gone. I will be with my Harold again, my legs will work again, and we will dance and sing and spin with happiness.

We had such happy times together. He was as good a husband as any girl could wish for, and when family didn't arrive, it just brought us even closer together. We were a team. We didn't do much socialising with other couples because we didn't fit in, not having children. It never really bothered us because we had each other. We were friendly with the neighbours, but it was mostly conversations over the garden fence or gate, so when Harold stopped in the garden, that all tailed off.

Harold's pipe still sits in the ashtray beside his chair. I never moved it after he died. Somehow, seeing it there makes it feel as if he is still here with me. Sometimes I chat to him, and we laugh at the funny things that happened to us. On the floor in front of the fire is the old rag rug that Harold made. My, it must be fifty years old now and probably accounts for a lot of the stale smell in the room even before my bladder opened. I remember him sitting here in the evenings making the rug, using bits of fabric leftover from any sewing I'd done. When it was new it had every colour under the sun in it. It was bright, and cheerful, and made with love, taking pride of place in the living room. Now the colours are faded and it's been trodden down so much that it's only half the depth it was, if even that. Being fabric, it has absorbed the smells of the room over the years. In the old days, I would take it outside, give it a good clean and hang it over the line to freshen up, but I don't think it's been outside for about 15 years. When Harold first died, I didn't want to wash it because I felt I would be washing away Harold's smells, the traces of his pipe tobacco, the earthy smell of the garden. And with my health problems, I don't think I've been out of the back door myself for about 8 years.

The flowered wallpaper is faded now but when we put it up together it was Rose Pink. Harold would always be drawn to anything that included my name. He would say "I just can't get enough Rose in my life." I always felt so treasured by him. We worked together decorating the walls – I would be chief labourer, doing the pasting at the table, and he was master-craftsman, applying the paper to the walls. We each knew our place in the team and it worked for us.

Looking now at Harold's chair, I can see a stain where his head would rest, the fabric marked by grease and sweat from his hair. At one time it would have frustrated me and I would have tried to renew the fabric as best I could. Now, I look at that stain and I see Harold, dozing in the early evening, a gentle snore coming from his open mouth.

On the window sill stands an empty vase. It's been empty for at least five years. When Harold was alive it was never without flowers. Roses of course, from the garden, late Spring to early Autumn, and over the other months he would bring me whichever flowers were in season. The house always had the sweet fragrance of the garden, and with my baking, it would often also have the wonderfully pleasing aroma of freshly baked bread, still warm from the oven. We didn't have many visitors, having no family, but if anybody did come they would always comment on the wonderful sensual experience of being in our home. Now it is just a shell – not a home anymore, in the truest sense. I feel like Miss Haversham, as if time has stopped and my life has ended, except I, unlike Miss Haversham, enjoyed fifty years of love and friendship with my wonderful man.

The last meal I had was three days ago, a ready meal of beef stew and mashed potatoes. My ready meals are delivered every fortnight from a local company. The friendly chap brings them to my door and I slowly make several trips back and forth to my kitchen to put them in the freezer. The milkman brings me bread and milk and a few other bits and pieces every week. I think he's due the day after tomorrow. It will probably be him who raises the alarm. I hope I'll be gone by then. Gary is a lovely chap and I'd hate for him to see me in this state. He's learnt over the years that it takes me a while to get to the door and he always waits patiently for me, ready for a little chat before going off on his way.

I have a little table beside my chair which is cluttered with all the things that I need to have close beside me. There are the dregs of an old cup of tea, the telephone, my address book, my glasses, my inhaler, my television remote and a, now empty, tablet case. The boxes of tablets are on the worktop in my kitchen. I would normally have refilled my tablet case for the day when I made my cup of tea at breakfast, but as I have been stuck in this chair, I've now missed several doses. I suppose that will just speed along the process.

I am beginning to feel very sleepy now. I'm not in any pain. My breathing is slow and relaxed. I do feel a bit cold and I can't quite reach the blanket on the arm of the sofa. Having my legs up on the stool makes it hard for me to reach forward, so I bring one of the cushions from behind my back and cuddle it against my front to try to warm up. Funny really, normally I can't get to sleep if I'm a bit cold. Harold used to laugh at me because in the middle of the night I would be throwing the covers off me, being too hot, and yet when I first got in bed I would always need extra warmth. The sun seems to have gone down now – I wonder what time it is? Thankfully, the curtains were already open before I got myself in this predicament so I have been able to enjoy the sun's warmth on my body during the day. I think I'll just close my eyes for a bit and have a rest.

**

"Can I take your name, sir?"

"It's Gary. I'm the Milkman. I do deliveries to Rose every week. I've been delivering to her for 5 years now."

"Does she have any family, to your knowledge?"

"I don't think so. I've never seen anybody but her, and the only person she ever talked about was her husband, who died a few years back."

"How was she when you came with your delivery last week?"

"Same as always. Slow, tired, but friendly. She's a lovely woman. I felt sorry for her. I'm not due for another couple of days but I was just passing and I felt like I should come and knock on. I'm glad I did now." Gary glanced to his left and saw the paramedics stepping out of the door, easing the stretcher over the threshold. As they met the clean, cool air they inhaled huge gulps, attempting to exhale the musty, stagnant air from their lungs. Rose was lying unconscious, with an oxygen mask over her face, oblivious to the commotion around her. The paramedics struggled to steer the stretcher along the winding path without being scratched by the thorny branches of the wild roses and cursed under their breath.

"I think the whole place needs gutting," said one of the paramedics.

"Yeah. I doubt she'll be ever be coming back here again. She'll probably go into a home after this. She obviously can't look after herself anymore, and she doesn't seem to have any family."

Rose was wheeled onto the ambulance and the policeman organised for the door to be boarded up. "No, I wouldn't bother going to too much trouble," he said to the faceless person on the other end of the phone, "she won't be coming back"

AWAKENING

Richie generally spent his days wearing his happiness like a veneer, like an inverted scratchboard where the coloured layer is on the outside. He knew exactly what he was doing but he could no longer help himself. He was addicted to performance, living his life as a character, so that now the lines between fake and real were blurred, even to himself.

At six foot two inches, he was hard to miss, even if you hadn't first been drawn by his slightly grating voice. His features had a delicate, effeminate character, prettier than a girl in full make-up. His skin was smooth and his nose perfectly formed; his dainty ears were intricately drawn and were edged by his flawlessly sculpted dark hair. He was slender of frame and in good physical health.

When Richie was the focus of peoples' attention, he could hold them in the palm of his hand like a court jester. He would assume his position, puff out his chest and entertain. His repertoire seemed endless and his energy unlimited, but once his audience had moved on, his hand would unconsciously rise to his lips and he would gnaw at his cuticles until they bled. A close examination of his hands would reveal his insecurities, that all was not as it seemed, but few people took the time to lower their gaze from his sparky and effervescent face.

He swept into the bar as if making a stage entrance, drawing attention from more than those who were expecting him.

'Hiya,' he called as he entered, '*Soooo* sorry I'm *laaate*.'

Richie kissed each of his friends on the cheek and squeezed himself onto the bench seat between two of the girls.

'That's ok, Richie, but we were beginning to think you weren't coming!'

'Of course I was coming. Wouldn't miss it for all the world, but there's always a crisis at my house. If one sister isn't being brought home by the police, the other sister is sitting quietly in a pool of blood! Never a dull day!'

Richie rolled his eyes and laughed. His friends took his lead and laughed along with him, assuming this was another example of the Richie hyperbole they knew and loved.

'effortful Well, it's good that you're here now. It's your round!' they laughed.

'Oooh, right. What's everybody having?'

With the requests ringing in his ears, Richie approached the bar. An attractive man in his thirties slid past him and Richie looked over his shoulder at the girls, widening his eyes and raising his eyebrows. Only one of the girls saw, the others having brought their heads together in discussion. Richie felt his spirits begin to plummet and began to unconsciously chew his cuticles while he concentrated on how he should regain their attention. He had noticed a slight cooling with the girls and was afraid they were getting bored with him. He needed to up the ante somehow. Their admiration was his lifeblood. Without that he was lost, and yet conversely, there was a part of him that craved being valued without the need to constantly please. It was consuming all his energy and he didn't know how to stop.

By the end of the evening, he was exhausted. It had been hard work to hold the attention of the girls tonight, even though he had utilised every flamboyant muscle in his bank. Waving goodbye to his friends, Richie began his journey home. He decided to walk as it was a mild night and he took the quieter route, away from the busier roads. He hadn't been walking long when he spotted a stationary wheelchair beside the railings of the park. As he approached, the occupant of the wheelchair, an elderly man wearing a light windcheater, turned his head and waved an arm at him, beckoning him forward. The man spoke but his words were slurred and effortful. Richie assumed he'd had a stroke and looked around to see if there was anybody with him. The man spoke again, gesturing to the wheelchair.

'Can....you....help...me?' the man said with great effort.

'Battery…. Dead'. He pointed down to his wheelchair.

'Oh no,' Richie replied, bending to meet the gentleman's eyes. 'Where do you need to go?'

'Ill….show….you.' The man pointed up the street ahead.

Richie noticed that the man was shivering.

'How long have you been stuck here?'

'About…..one…..hour.'

'How does this thing work anyway?' Richie started to push the chair and was surprised by the weight of it.

'By…..battery…..usually'. the man joked.

The two men made their way up the street, then Richie turned to the right as indicated. When told to cross the road, he swung the wheelchair around immediately, moving towards the curb.

'Noooo…….noooo.' shouted the man, flapping his arm, 'Not….here! …..Too….steep!'

'Ooops', said Richie with a giggle, 'that was close!'

It took about ten minutes to reach the man's home, which had a ramp up to the front door. As the gentleman brought his keys from his pocket, he looked at Richie then nodded his head towards the door, 'Come….in.'

Richie pushed the wheelchair over the threshold and looked around him. The wallpaper was faded and curling up at the seams. The carpet was littered with detritus, bits of paper, food crumbs, junk mail. He wheeled the chair into the living room. The sofa was piled high with books and boxes. A small trolley stood at one end of the sofa, its surface covered with tablet boxes, remote controls, and envelopes. Another wheelchair, without a battery, occupied the space at the other end and the man gestured for Richie to wheel him to it. As he transferred from one wheelchair to the other Richie was able to see how severely the stroke had disabled him. His right arm hung limp and heavy, fingers so swollen that they looked like well-stuffed sausages; Moving his right leg was an effort, and his toes sloped down to the floor when he picked up his leg. His movements were laboured and clumsy, but once in the lighter wheelchair, he was able to propel himself slowly by peddling with his feet.

'Would you like me to make you a hot drink before I leave you?' asked Richie.

'Yes……please…….coffee…..milk…..no sugar.'

The kitchen was not large and Richie wondered how the man managed to negotiate his wheelchair in there. He assumed there must be carers involved, as the kitchen was in a much better state than the living room, with all the worktops clean and tidy.

'Let….me…..give……you something…..for your…..trouble.' the man said, fumbling with his wallet, trying to get some money out.

'No way,' said Richie, 'I'm happy to help.'

His eyes took in the photographs around the walls, happy, smiling photographs of the man with crowds of people surrounding him, possibly in Africa, judging by the smiling black faces and the landscape in the background. Then he spotted a smaller photograph on the bureau, featuring not just the gentleman but also the Queen! Beside the photograph was a case with a cross-like medal on a red ribbon, with a newspaper cutting tucked into the opposite side of the case. The headline read 'OBE awarded to Norman Reynolds for his charity work in Kenya'.

'Wow, you have an OBE? Can I have a closer look, please?'

'Of…..course.' Norman said.

The article spoke of Norman's work in Kenya, schools built and resourced for hundreds of children. He had set up a charity in 1979 when he was in his early thirties and had received his OBE in 2006. Richie was impressed at the selflessness of this man who seemed to have dedicated his life to helping others.

'Your family must be so proud of you,' he said, glancing around the pictures to find photographs of a wife, children, grandchildren.

'No…..family…….That…….was……my life……All……gone….Alone…….now.'

Richie felt saddened that a man who had given so much to so many people should now be alone in the world.

Impulsively he asked 'Can I come back and visit you, Norman? I'd love to get to know you more, hear your stories about Africa.'

A lop-sided grin came to Norman's face, and his eyes filled.

'I'd….like….that.'

Richie had an extra bounce to his step as he continued his journey home. He was filled with admiration and respect for Norman, and also with sadness at the disappointing end to the life of such an exceptional human being. He resolved to be a friend to Norman and to help him in any way he could.

The following weekend Richie arrived bearing cake and the two men spent an afternoon getting to know each other better. Norman taught Richie how to play chess, and though the conversation was slow due to Norman's slurred speech, they developed an easy understanding of each other. Each of them began to look forward to their weekend meetings, venturing further afield to the local parks and canal tow-paths to soak up the sunshine.

One weekend Richie began to clear the floors and push a hoover around, a la Freddie Mercury, whilst singing "I want to break free", bringing loud guffaws from Norman, and then he turned up the next weekend with decorating tools, proceeding, with Norman's permission, to strip the curling wallpaper. Together they chose some new paper which Richie applied, transforming the whole room. While Richie worked, Norman told him about Kenya, about the families living in poverty, and the importance of education to give the children opportunities to better themselves. Norman's speech seemed to be less arduous the more opportunity he had to use his voice. Once the decorating was finished, Richie helped to declutter the house and found that Norman had a story behind every item. Richie was enthralled at the full life Norman had lived, which seemed very exotic in comparison to his life in the North West. As Norman's speech increased, Richie found his own lessened considerably. He was quite happy not being at the centre of the story, he loved to listen, to marvel at the experience of somebody other than himself. When he met up with his friends in the evenings, a little less often than he used to, he found that he no longer craved their attention, and found himself, instead, telling them about his new friend.

It was early November when Richie had the call from the hospital. Norman had named him as next of kin when he was taken in by ambulance. He had suffered another stroke, and then another, this time catastrophic, and within a couple of days, he had lost his battle. The nurse told Richie that Norman's bag was still on the ward and requested that he collect it as soon as he was able. Shocked and upset, Richie made his way to the hospital.

Norman had always carried with him a large rucksack which he attached to his electric wheelchair. Richie had often joked that he looked like he carried everything *including* the kitchen sink with him, but Norman would not go anywhere without it. After he had collected it from the ward, Richie sat in the car and opened the bag. Inside was an old-fashioned tape recorder machine, with a cassette inside it already. Ejecting the tape, Richie was surprised to find his name written on it, "For Richie". Returning it to the machine he pressed 'Play' and heard Norman's voice...

'Richie,

Meeting you.... on that path.... late at night when.... the battery went..... on my wheelchair..... was the best thing that has happened..... to me since my life..... was..... devastated.... by my first stroke......Before you, I would go..... weeks without..... seeing people..... unless I went out.... onto the.... High Street..... Before you..... nobody had stepped.... over my doorstep... for more than two.... years.

Being able to.....relive my.... history..... as I talked to you..... has brought joy back.... into my life..... You are a good.... lad with a heart.... of gold,..... and I have been..... honoured.... to have you as.... my friend...... But I have sensed...... unhappiness...... in you,..... behind that sunny..... personality,..... as if you haven't..... quite found out.... who you are yet,....what your purpose.... is.

I hope you find it..... Son,..... you have a lot..... to give, and I have..... certainly..... appreciated all that..... you have done for me..... – not only the..... practical things,..... but your friendship too.

I had to record...... this over..... several sessions..... – waiting for me to..... make a speech..... like this would have..... seen your hair.... turn grey before.... my eyes! But I..... wanted to say ......it because..... I love you, lad.

Don't just...... dream your..... dreams – live them........ I'll be with you..... all the way."

Richie placed his hand tenderly on the cassette player as the tears rolled down his face.

'I will, Norman, I will,' he whispered, 'thank you '.

Over the next few weeks, as he packed away Norman's things, Richie began to dream of getting on a plane and flying to Kenya. He scoured the various papers in Norman's house and managed to find some names and addresses, and he hoped that at least some of them would still be traceable. He then made the leap, resigning from his job and buying a ticket to Nairobi, before he had a chance to change his mind.

He explained his plans to his friends, who were shocked but excited for him. He had discovered over recent months that he didn't need to perform anymore, that he didn't need to be happy all of the time. His friends had seen how his new friendship with Norman had brought out a sensitivity that had previously been hidden by his need for affirmation. Richie had discovered that it was in giving of oneself to others that one can feel good about oneself, and that, only in recognising his own worth, would he find true happiness.

As he ascended the steps to the aircraft, he tapped his pocket and felt the case containing Norman's OBE.

'This is for you, Norman, and for me'.

ARTIFICIAL INTELLIGENCE

Monday

This is what she wants most in the world, and that is precisely why I cannot allow her to have it. She has fed us lies for years about her perfect life and perfect marriage; her perfectly beautiful face has haunted me, looking out from school photographs and later from the tabloids, as she lived her life in the full glare of the paparazzi.

I saw the interview on television today. Only Blaire Mortisson would have the nerve to use a televised interview to reach out to her old school friends like that. What was wrong with social media or the other methods that we mere mortals would use to contact old friends.

'It's been such a terrible time for me, and I'm relieved that it's now all over.' She said.

'When you married Kyle 25 years ago, he was already a well-known sportsman. Were there signs of substance abuse back then? Did you not have an inkling of the way that things may progress?'

'I was so young then. I'd had a very sheltered life. I knew nothing about the misuse of alcohol or drugs, or what it could do to someone's personality. Of course, we would have a drink to

celebrate with friends but he was gentle and protective towards me and he made me feel very special, treasured even.'

'How long into your marriage did that change?'

'After about ten years his dependence upon various substances had become all-consuming. If I said anything to him, he would lash out in anger. Just verbally at first, but then it became increasingly physical.'

So, why were you still gurning for the cameras with him for another fifteen years then? Rubbing our faces in your shallow happiness and perfect life? Making us feel less with every picture of you printed in the press …

'I now realise that I put my whole life and faith in the hands of somebody who abused that trust. It's made me reflect on what is important in life. Family and friendships. When I was at school I had the most wonderful group of girlfriends. I let their friendships slip when I got with Kyle, but I'd so love to get together with them again. I'm feeling battered and bruised and in need of a bit of girl power," she smiled through tearful eyes at the camera, "so if you're out there Emma, Ava, and Charlotte, please get in touch. Oh, and Mia too, of course.'

There I go, an afterthought, on the periphery as always. Nothing has changed.

I take out the old, faded school photograph which I look at virtually every day, and peer at the grainy image of my teenage self - in the photograph but to the side, only just in the frame. The faces of the four other girls are beaming as they pose their bodies, arms draped over each other. She is in the centre of the picture of course, holding court, leading the charge, orchestrating the actions of the rest of the crowd. I am present but stand in the shadows, looking on – a spectator of the scene rather than a player. There is something sick in my obsession with this photo. I have no need of using a blade on some hidden part of my body for release, I simply take out the photo and pick at the wound, refusing to allow it to heal. This image provides me with my daily dose of pain, proving that I am alive.

The eye is drawn immediately to the slim, blonde girl in the centre – hair long and silky even in the battered photograph. She is looking straight into the camera, honing her skills for her later relationship with the paparazzi of the world, confident and very much in control of the image she is portraying. She has her arms draped around Ava and Emma; Ava has short dark hair with a curl; she is funny and knows how to bring everybody into uncontrollable laughter, though she often does this in a fairly quiet way. She is not showy but her humour has endeared her to all and she is very much in the centre. Emma, with longer, curly hair is kind. She has a maternal instinct which means that everybody feels cared for. In the photograph she is turning slightly, bringing her head round in my direction. I think she is trying to draw me into the picture, but I remain detached, one step removed. Next to Ava is Charlotte, short, blonde bob, trendy in her high shine fabrics and neat figure. You see, everybody had a role to play in 'our gang', each had their own place, be it humour, kindness or trend-setting, but what was my role? My speciality was my ability to cut through the crap, and this wasn't always welcomed by the rest of the group.

And yet I needed them. They were the only family I had. My mother was nothing more than a face looking out from a photograph; I felt detached from her, she meant nothing to me. My dad didn't go in much for demonstrations of affection. He made sure that I had food, and shelter, and what I needed for school, but that was the extent of his attention. Very young, I decided that I needed to create my own family. They always say you can't choose your family, but I did. I learnt to play the game, how to make people like me by giving them what they wanted – just the right mix of ego-stroking and charisma. I was never the centre of the pack, but I could pretend that I belonged and that was enough for me, to begin with.

People have asked me when I was at my happiest but I can't answer that question. What is happiness? I don't think I have tasted it. In fact, I think happiness is the trait I find most unbearable in other people. Nauseating happiness. Pushing their happiness into your face. People who live their lives in some other-worldly state of cheesy cheerfulness. I want to show them how ugly the world really is, and how ugly people really are. People let you down, you can't trust them. The world is full of selfishness and misery, pain and misunderstanding – if you can't see that you are blind or deluded.

So, back to Blaire's pathetic request for all her girlfriends to gather around her in her moment of need. Blaire needs to be taught a lesson. She needs to see the world as it really is. And she needs to value honesty, after all her years of dishonesty.

***

Monday

Ava rushed through the front door out of the rain. Her hair was already a write-off and had turned into candy-floss, such was the frizz in her short curls. Placing the shopping bags on the counter she sighed as she spotted that her son's muddy football kit was in a heap in the middle of the kitchen floor.

'Sam, get down here and put this stuff in the washing machine,' she shouted up the stairs. Hearing the base of the music vibrating off the walls and the door of his bedroom she sighed again and scooped up the clothes herself.

Turning on the radio while she prepared the evening meal she paused when she heard the reporter say 'The high profile divorce of Kyle Fisher and Blaire Mortisson has finally concluded, with Blaire being awarded £1 million for every year they were married. That's quite a paycheck after 25 years of marriage for Ms Mortisson. Earlier, in an interview for CNN Ms Mortissen said this.....

'I knew nothing about the misuse of alcohol or drugs, or what it could do to someone's personality. Of course, we would have a drink to celebrate with friends but he was gentle and protective towards me and he made me feel very special, treasured even.'

'How long into your marriage did that change?'

'After about ten years his dependence upon various substances had become all-consuming. If I said anything to him, he would lash out in anger. Just verbally at first, but then it became increasingly physical.'

Sam wandered into the room, head down to his mobile phone, tapping away with his thumbs on the screen. A rush of emotion overcame Ava as she looked at her son, her miracle child, conceived after five bouts of IVF. Turning to him she asked

'How did the match go?'

'Good, yeah. I scored! We won 3-2.' He grinned, putting his phone into the pocket of his ripped jeans.

'That's brilliant' Ava said, resisting the urge to proudly hug her son. She was learning to navigate that difficult road of parenting a teenage son, where physical demonstrations of affection were spurned and interest in his life needed to appear low-key. Turning away she began to unpack the shopping.

'Spaghetti bolognaise for tea tonight. I bet you're starving, are you? Or did you drop off for a burger on the way home?'

'Well, I did, yeah,' he smiled, 'but I'm still starving!'

Ava grinned, shaking her head, 'Teenage boys! There's no filling them.'

Later that evening Ava was surprised when the telephone rang at 8.30 pm.

'Hi Ava, it's Mia. How are you? I hope you don't mind me ringing you. It's just that I've been thinking about you recently so I thought I'd give you a call.'

'Oh, hi Mia. It's great to hear from you. It's been a while.'

Ava tried to calculate how long it had been since she had

spoken to Mia. It must have been around the time that Sam was born. Yes, the school reunion, 10 years after they had finished Sixth Form. She seemed to remember that Mia had moved away, to the Midlands she thought.

'The last time I saw you, you looked about to burst!' Mia said, with a laugh in her voice. 'I thought you were going to give birth right there in the old school hall!'

It was as if Mia was reading her thoughts.

'Haha, yes. Well, he's a seventeen-year-old giant now, eating me out of house and home! How are you, Mia? What are you up to nowadays?'

'Oh, you know, same old, same old. Speaking of old – did you see our old friend on TV today? Blaire's divorce has come through and she's made a pretty packet.'

'I heard something about it on the radio, but then Sam came in so I didn't catch it all. She sounded like she's had a hard time of it.'

'Yeah, I think so. I wondered whether it would be nice to have a bit of a shindig for old time's sake. I don't mind doing all the organising, but obviously, I wouldn't be able to host it from down here. Charlotte's in a flat and I think Emma's girlfriend might get a bit jealous of all the girlies getting together, so I wondered if we could have it at yours?'

Ava hesitated, looking around at her home, which was in desperate need of a lick of paint and some new furniture. Blaire was loaded – she probably lived in a pristine mansion, filled with the highest class, bespoke furniture.

'What Blaire needs at the moment is her old friends – she's not going to be worried about what somewhere looks like.'

Ava wasn't sure whether to be insulted or reassured by Mia's words, but, as usual, Mia seemed to have been reading her mind.

'Er, yes, that would be fine. I'd need to run it by Eddie, of course, but he works away so much that he probably wouldn't even notice.'

'That's what I figured. That's great, thanks, Ava. Shall we say next Saturday evening then? I'll sort everything out, don't worry.'

'Er, ...'

'Take care then, Ava, and see you soon.'

Ava replaced the telephone into its cradle in a bit of a daze. Wow, Mia was always a tour de force when she set her mind to something. No change there then. She smiled to herself –

maybe Sam would be impressed that his boring old mother was friends with a celebrity, a very attractive celebrity at that. She was relieved that Mia had taken on all the organisation – that meant she could concentrate on getting the house into some sort of order, and then look forward to seeing all her friends again. Over the years they had drifted apart, not because of any animosity, but life had merely taken them in different directions. She knew that Charlotte was working in the city somewhere but had lost touch, and Emma had moved away when she set up home with her girlfriend following a surprising divorce from her husband. For a moment Ava wondered how Mia knew where to find everyone, but then she had always been watchful, more an observer than a participant in their friendship group. It kind of made sense that she might have continued to watch and keep track of their activities over the years, and, though that thought did send a shiver through Ava, she didn't dwell on it.

***

Tuesday

Charlotte no longer owned a television. She had given up as much of her 'stuff' as she possibly could so she could commit herself to her work. She had felt a hypocrite to be helping those who had nothing when she herself had so much.

Since her earliest memories she had loved fashion; saving

every penny that she had to ensure that she could purchase the latest styles, and she had always bought quality. She expressed her personality through the clothes that she wore and the clothes gave her confidence. She was very aware during her teenage years that she had been envied by many of the other girls because her neat figure and long legs were perfect for whichever style she chose. Designers always created their work based on the tall, skinny models that would show them off to the world and Charlotte had been blessed with a similar figure.

Now this all seemed rather shallow and she was ashamed to remember her misguided priorities. About ten years ago she had seen an advert asking for donations to raise money for girls who could not afford a wedding dress for their big day. This had coincided with her having a good clear out of her wardrobe, and she had many retro outfits in immaculate condition which she no longer planned to keep. It seemed serendipitous that she should see the advert at this time and she had gone along to the church with her donations. The people she had met there were inspirational. They could see others in need and were doing something practical about it; not only that, but they weren't doing it to make themselves feel good or for any reward – their reward was in building connections with people and bringing a degree of joy to them. Charlotte had quickly established herself as one of the group and had found it to be life-changing. Her outlook on life was transformed. She had gradually reduced her wardrobe to only what was necessary and now found herself shopping for outfits in the charity shops. She had discovered that she could create her own designs with a bit of imagination, and was able to help other women to do the same. What could be picked up in a charity shop had been an eye-opener and she now accompanied women to the stores, helping them to create their own wardrobes, assembling a few garments that could be worn in different ways and in different combinations. The difference this had made to the esteem of these unfortunate woman had been a revelation and Charlotte had been humbled.

She had sold her house and moved into a smallish flat. The spare room was used as a store of used clothing for those who had absolutely nothing and could not even afford the charity shop prices. She had donated half of the money from the sale of her house to the shelter offering support for women escaping domestic abuse. Her days were full, meeting the women and taking them shopping; her evenings were full, mending the slight flaws in the items she stocked, or ironing them so that they looked in the best possible condition for women who had nothing else. Seeing the rise in the self-esteem of the women gave her the best reward she could imagine, as they stepped forward into their new life, and she dropped into bed like a stone each night after an exhausting but satisfying day.

Charlotte was surprised when she entered the church hall to find Mia waiting for her. She hadn't seen Mia for years. She was wearing reflective sunglasses, so it was hard to see how the years had changed her, but Charlotte recognised the slightly clenched jaw in the smile that greeted her. She had sometimes thought that Mia's jaw was not unlike that of a Staffordshire bull terrier, which the popular myth says once it has locked its jaw around your leg, is unable to open it again. Charlotte felt ashamed of this thought, raised her eyes for forgiveness, and approached Mia with arms held wide for a hug. She felt tension in Mia as she embraced her, and sought to help her to relax.

'Let's go and have a brew in the back room.'

Mia followed, taking in Charlotte's still girlish figure and the stylish way that it was dressed. 'She's still got it,' she thought.

'Fancy seeing you after all this time!' Charlotte smiled. 'How did you even know where to find me?'

'Oh, it wasn't so hard.' Mia said, 'You're talked about quite a lot around here you know. All the work you do for these women. You're quite the Mother Theresa, but with better style!'

Charlotte smiled, quelling the instinctive discomfort that she was feeling. Was she imagining a hint of bitterness in that quip from Mia? Of course she was. Why would Mia come all this way to see her if it wasn't out of sincere motives?

Mia gazed at Charlotte through her tinted glasses; she smelt the uncertainty in Charlotte. She knew that on this visit she would need to be more careful. Of all the girls, Charlotte was the most likely to suspect Mia's true motives – that was why she had decided to wear the sun-glasses, so that she could remain veiled as much as possible. She could see the battle going on within Charlotte and hoped that her more recent 'holier than thou' side would triumph now that she was involved with the church.

'Did you hear about Blaire? She got her divorce through. She was on the telly yesterday.'

'Oh, no, I didn't hear. I'm so caught up here I never hear much of the news. Poor Blaire. How is she? Have you seen her?'

'No, I haven't seen her yet, but I did speak to Ava. She's thinking of hosting a bit of a get-together for us all, so we can gather around Blaire and support her. What do you think?'

Charlotte thought for a moment and Mia could see that she was thinking of her old friend.

'Would you come? On Saturday? At Ava's? Here's the address. It will just be the 5 of us, like old times.'

Charlotte took the piece of paper Mia held out. 'Of course

I'll come. Poor Blaire. I've not thought about her for years. The last time I saw a picture of her in the paper she looked really happy with her husband.'

'Yes, well, that was just a smoke-screen, apparently. But she's loaded now – maybe she could donate something to your ladies here.'

Charlotte looked at Mia, a little shocked that she should be talking in such a mercenary manner under the circumstances. But she did have a point. Blaire must have so many outfits that she could donate, sell, auction. The difference it would make would be amazing. And seeing all the girls would be good.

'Great, well, I'll see you Saturday then. Thanks Mia.'

***

Wednesday

'We've had another couple of those funny calls, Emm'

Emma sighed. 'Kirsten, I've told you. I don't know who it could be. Please believe me.'

She walked towards Kirsten and wrapped her arms around her.

'You know I love you. Why would I need to see anyone

else? I'm perfectly happy as I am.'

Kirsten stiffened in her arms., refusing to respond to her touch.

'Well, it's you she keeps asking for. And whenever I ask who she is, she puts the phone down. Today she sounded like she'd been crying when she spoke.'

'Just don't answer it and she'll get fed up, whoever she is. Let the answer-machine pick up, and if you hear her voice, hang up.'

'That's not the point. I still want to know who she is and why she rings you all the time.'

'And I don't have an answer to that. What gets me is why she always seems to ring when I'm not around. The time she rings when I am, I'll give her a piece of my mind.'

Emma plopped down on the sofa in frustration. She had only ever loved two people in her life. Her husband, Terry, whom she had married young when not long out of school, and then Kirsten, who she had met at work. Leaving Terry had been the toughest decision of her life. She still cared for him deeply. She had simply fallen in love with somebody else, and that somebody else happened to be a woman, which had seemed to hurt Terry all the more as he felt that their marriage had been a sham. Had she always known she was a lesbian, he had shouted. Had she merely been pretending that he gave her any kind of pleasure? No, she had replied, I am not a lesbian, I have just fallen in love with a woman. Yes, of course you gave me pleasure, everything in our marriage was real. It's not that I have changed, I've simply fallen in love with somebody else. I still love you, care for you, but I don't think I'm in love with you anymore. Thankfully, there had not been any children to disrupt and she had packed her bags and left.

Kirsten was a quiet and softly spoken woman, the gentlest creature she had ever known. She was kind and thoughtful, but she was also sensitive, highly strung. Emma needed to be the strong one in their relationship, calming Kirsten's anxieties, which tended to overwhelm her on occasions. Twelve months ago, the anxiety had reached a crisis point and Emma was at her wit's end. She'd managed to persuade the doctor to prescribe some sedatives for Kirsten and had seen an almost immediate improvement. The anxiety symptoms reduced dramatically but Kirsten had come to depend on them more and more. A couple of months ago she had been looking for something and gone into Kirsten's bedside cabinet and been shocked to find a stock of strong painkillers. She'd asked where they had come from and Kirsten had seemed a bit secretive when answering, but Kirsten's mood swings were becoming more dramatic and she was becoming a little paranoid sometimes. She was now fixating on these telephone calls, which Emma felt were not happening as often as she was suggesting, if they were happening at all. Working nights was not helping as she wasn't able to keep the eye on Kirsten that she would like. She was exhausted and needed to go to bed. As she stood to make her way to the bedroom, the intercom rang. She pressed the button

'Hello?'

'Oh hi. Is that Emma? It's Mia. Mia, from school. Is it a good time?'

Mia? Wow, that was a blast from the past! What could she be wanting? Emma tried to remember the last time she'd had contact with Mia. Was it around the time she left Terry? She seemed to remember bumping into Mia in a coffee shop. She'd just left Terry and met with Kirsten to tell her that she had finally done it, and they could begin to plan a life together. Kirsten had left the coffee shop to go to work and Emma had remained at the table, crushed with the emotion of her actions. Mia had suddenly appeared before her as if from nowhere, and it had been so good to have the company of an old friend. She had told Mia the whole story and Mia had listened so patiently. She hadn't shown any shock or judgement, but then Emma remembered that Mia had always kept her own counsel. It never had been easy to know what was going through her mind. Emma had always felt protective towards Mia, feeling that she either lacked the confidence to fully engage with people, or she had erected an invisible barrier around herself, maybe because she felt vulnerable. Well, it wasn't great timing that she had arrived now, just as Emma had finished a night shift, but she was here, so what could she do but let her in. She buzzed for the locked door to open.

Seconds later a slightly breathless Mia stood in front of her at the door.

'Wow, those stairs are a bit of a workout, aren't they? No wonder you still look so great!'

'Mia,' Emma smiled, then embraced her old friend. 'It's great to see you. I must look awful though – I'm working nights at the moment and haven't even had time to change. Forgive this state.' She said, motioning to her nurse's uniform. 'What brings you here? And how did you find me? We hadn't got this flat the last time I saw you.'

'I just took a punt! I thought I saw you a few weeks ago when I was passing on a bus. You were struggling with some shopping, but you were fumbling at this door. I saw someone coming out just now and asked which was your flat. I hope you don't mind. Oh, hi – you must be Kirsten?'

Mia gave a friendly wave to Kirsten who had come to see who Emma was speaking to. Mia's gaze settled on Kirsten just a little longer to see if she recognised her. No, she was safe. She had always been very careful to cover all her hair in a hat when she passed over the tablets and to wear the heavy framed glasses.

'Yes, this is Kirsten. I can't believe you remembered her name! Your memory is amazing. Come on in. It's lovely to see you.'

As Mia settled herself on the sofa she swung her long hair so that it fell forward, slightly obscuring her features on Kirsten's side.

'Mia and I were friends at school. There were five of us that hung around together all the time.....'

'And that's why I'm here actually. Did you hear about Blaire? Her divorce? It's been all over the news lately.'

'You're joking, aren't you? When I'm on nights I just come home, flop into bed, then back to work again the next day. I haven't seen the news in weeks. Poor Blaire, I wondered whether she would be truly happy with Kyle. All that press attention, all those girls throwing themselves at her famous husband.'

'Hmm, drugs apparently. He was addicted to all sorts – cocaine, prescription tablets.....'

Mia let her gaze settle on Kirsten for a moment.

'I think I have a headache, actually. Nice to meet you, Mia.' Kirsten got up and left the room. Mia smiled inwardly; it was just too easy with Kirsten, like a cat toying with a bird, torturing it mercilessly before going in for the kill.

'Anyway, I heard from Ava the other day, and she's planning a bit of a do for her to cheer her up. Everybody's going to be there apparently. Come along, bring Kirsten.'

'I'll have to look at my shifts. I can't remember if I'm working. Hang on a minute.'

Mia, knowing that Emma was not working having secured that information before suggesting Saturday to Ava, sat back on the sofa while Emma found her phone to check her shifts. She spied a piece of paper which had fallen from Emma's pocket – a list of all her patients on the ward and her nurses' scribble beside each one denoting tasks to be completed with each one. She slipped it into her pocket. A sample of Emma's writing would be a useful aide later.

'Yes, I am free that night, so I'll be there. It will be lovely to see everyone again. I'm not sure if Kirsten will be there or not. I don't think she's very well at the moment.'

'Oh dear. What's wrong? Can I help?'

'To be honest I'm getting really worried about her. She's relying a bit too much on some sedatives the doctor gave her, and now she seems to be stockpiling painkillers. She's acting very paranoid. She's convinced I'm having an affair. Keeps talking about some woman phoning all the time. "

'I'm sorry to hear that Emma. Substance abuse can get such a terrible grip on somebody. I hope nobody's going to think you're getting her the tablets from work. Having access to all those drugs on the ward, at night, when the ward is quiet.'

Emma raised her head quickly and looked at Mia. The thought had never occurred to her. Surely nobody would think that, would they? She didn't think she's confided in anyone other than Mia about her concerns so far. Perhaps it would be better not to. To deal with this on her own.

Mia saw that her tactic had worked and rose to take her leave.

'Well, I'd better let you get to bed. Great to see you, Emma. I'll see you Saturday.'

Giving Emma a peck on the cheek, she left the flat, grinning now that the first part of her plan had been completed. Now for Blaire.

***

Thursday

'Hi, Mrs Mortisson. I don't know whether you remember me. My name is Mia and I was friends with Blaire at school, along with Emma, Ava and Charlotte.'

Mrs Mortisson cast her mind back twenty-five years, yes, there was a group of them. Mostly pleasant girls, but there was one amongst them that was always rather sullen, a bit shifty. But she could never remember which was which – young girls were all make-up, hair, and hormones. Who knew what was going on in their minds.

'Oh yes, I remember you all coming around to the house, though you would disappear into Blaire's room and we never saw you all night, just heard the shrieks of laughter and the music playing.'

'Sorry Mrs M. I don't suppose you enjoyed having your house invaded! I saw the news earlier in the week, about Blaire. How is she doing? It was awful to hear all that she'd been going through.'

'Yes, it's been a dreadful time for her. I never liked Kyle, I can say that now. But she never even told me what was going on for all these years. I would have got her out of that marriage years ago if I'd known.'

'The thing is, she said something about seeing all her old friends in the interview on Monday. So, I've managed to get round to all the girls and we're having a get-together for Blaire on Saturday. Just a quiet evening of her closest friends, so we can show her we're there for her whenever she needs us. I'm finding it hard to get past her security to let her know. Please could you let her know? Saturday, at Ava's house. Seven-thirty in the evening.'

Mia gave Ava's address and hung up.

***

Saturday: 6.30pm

I arrive at Ava's loaded with bottles of wine, spirits, and mixers. When the door is opened by Eddie I am slightly taken aback. Damn, he was supposed to be working. I had carefully arranged my pieces on the board and had worked all my moves with precision. He was not part of my game plan.

'Hi, I'm Mia. I think Ava's expecting me?'

Eddie opened the door wider, but not wide enough, so that I needed to brush against his body to enter the house. He smiled at me and offered to help carry the bottles, which I happily gave to him, just so I knew where his hands were apart from anything else.

66

'Ava's in the kitchen.'

I could see that Ava had worked hard on the house preparing for tonight. She was dressed in new jeans and a pretty top, and the table was loaded with food.

'Wow,' I said, 'Someone's been busy!'

Hearing a sniff from my right I turned my head just as Eddie removed his hand from his trousers. My skin crawled as I saw his eyes travel over my body and his gaze hold mine just a little longer than necessary. Ava was busy with preparations and oblivious to her husband's inappropriate body language.

'I hope you won't mind us taking over your home for the evening, Eddie. I imagine you'll be glad for the opportunity to go out for a drink with the boys!' I said lightly. 'Strictly girls only tonight!'

'Yes, I've made that clear, Mia' said Ava, giving Eddie a look that sent him from the room for his coat. 'Sam's at his friend's til about 11 pm'.

With Eddie out of the way and Ava still busy, I was able to slip upstairs unnoticed. I crept into Ava's bedroom and took the scrapbook from my bag, placing it underneath the corner of the bed.

7.45 pm

'I'm feeling quite nervous, are you?' Emma asked, 'Do you think she'll have changed much? She's been living in a totally different world than the rest of us all these years.'

Kirsten surveyed Emma quietly, trying to assess whether this was Emma covering her lies. Why had she even brought her tonight? Was she just wanting to hurt her, humiliate her in front of her old school friends?

'But you said she wanted to meet with us, didn't you, Mia?' Charlotte asked. 'In the interview?'

'Yes, she did.'

'Well, I just hope she doesn't think my house is a dump. I've done the best I can, with the short notice I've had.'

The doorbell rang and we all rose to our feet. Ava opened the door and there stood Blaire, her father still seated in the car. She waved him off and stepped inside, a huge grin spreading across her face, looking at us each in turn.

'Oh my goodness, I can't believe it. Look at you all.'

After much hugging and kissing, we settled in the lounge, drinks in hand, and each began to tell our stories: what we had made of our lives, the decisions we had made, and the ripples that had spread from those decisions. The wine flowed as freely as the conversation, and after a while, more private conversations began to take place in smaller groupings. When I saw Kirsten rise to refill her drink in the kitchen, I followed her in.

'Kirsten, Emma asked me to slip this to you when we had a private moment.'

Handing her the folded slip of paper, I turned to fill my glass. Kirsten read the note, her hands shaking.

Kirsten,

I know you must be feeling a little on the outside this evening as this is the first time you have met these old friends of mine. I brought you here to show you how much I love you, and so that you can see how much better than these people you are, most especially this pretentious monstrosity that dear old Blaire has become. Where you are real, she is fake; you are gentle and sincere but she is merely a façade, a pretence, something shallow, window dressing. There is nothing of substance about her. It would be impossible for me to feel anything but scorn for her.

Please believe me, I mean this with all my heart.

Ems

Forging the letter in Emma's handwriting had been a

challenge, but the patient list I had procured from her flat had served me well. I could see that Kirsten had no doubts. A weak smile fluttered across her lips and she put the note in her pocket. I handed Kirsten the drink I had prepared, containing alcohol so that it would react nicely with the drugs already in her system, and awaited her response as the evening progressed.

10 pm

Following Blaire upstairs a few minutes after she had gone to the bathroom, I retrieved the scrapbook from underneath the bed. Positioning myself on the edge of the bed, with the bedroom door ajar, I waited for Blaire to come out. On hearing the door open I gasped loudly, and said, 'Oh no, no, Ava, how could you?'

The door opened slightly and Blaire peered in...

'Are you ok, Mia? What's up?'

I quickly shut the book as if to prevent Blaire from seeing it, fumbled and dropped the book at her feet.

'Don't, Blaire. Don't look at it. There must be an explanation, I'm sure.'

Blaire sat beside me on the bed and opened the book. It was filled with pictures of Blaire. Newspaper cuttings, magazine cuttings, Blaire's face on every page. But in each picture, the eyes had been gouged out roughly. Nasty slurs were written in red ink beside some of the pictures, vitriolic comments which spoke of hatred and jealousy.

'Where did you find it?' Blaire asked, just about holding her tears.

'I walked in thinking this was the bathroom. This was on the floor, as if it had been flung down in anger. The pages were open so I could see what it contained as soon as I saw it. How could she do this to you? How hateful. How two-faced, all this pretence this evening, when this is what she is really feeling. Oh Blaire, I'm so sorry.'

'Can you leave me alone for a minute, Mia? Please?'

I clasped her hand in mine, then left her sitting alone, the hate-filled scrapbook which I had cultivated for many years on her lap.

Downstairs I could see that the alcohol was working Kirsten up nicely into a state of agitation.

'Where's Emma?' she asked when I entered the room.

'Oh, I think I saw her upstairs just now, with Blaire.' I said breezily.

Alone in the room, I took out my mobile and sent the text to the reporter that I had prepared, pretending to be Charlotte, promising a great photo opportunity of Blaire Mortisson.

Emma, Charlotte and Ava remained in the garden, chatting while Charlotte sucked on her e-cigarette. I moved to the bottom of the stairs and heard Kirsten's voice…

'So, you see, I know it's been you that has been constantly calling the house. I know you want to bring all your little gang together again, but if you really want to know what they think of you, just read this. Emma wrote me this letter. Read it and you'll know what she really thinks of you and you can stop ringing our bloody phone!'

Smiling, I retreated to the garden to join the others.

'Hi, so this is where you all got to!'

'Hi Mia, we thought you must be with Blaire.' Said Charlotte.

'No, I'm not really sure where she is, to be honest. I thought she was out here with you guys.'

'Have you seen Kirsten, Mia?'

'Yes, she's fallen asleep on the sofa, bless her.'

So, when Blaire rushed from the house ten minutes later, we were not there to witness the confrontation with the reporter and photographer awaiting her exit.

'Blaire, is it true that you have refused to help fund the rescue charity for victims of domestic abuse. We have it on good authority from one of the volunteers that you have been approached about auctioning one of your dresses and you have refused. Don't you think that's a bit hypocritical, given that you have been a victim of domestic abuse yourself? Do you have any comment to make?'

Startled by the reporter and the flash of the camera Blaire stumbled forward, not seeing the lights of the oncoming car.

The sound of her body hitting the metalwork brought vomit to Sam's mouth. He sat in the car, stunned as the reporter and photographer leaned over the limp body of his mother's friend. It had all happened so quickly. Sam watched as the men rose again, turned to face him, and shook their heads. She was dead.

Kirsten screamed from the doorway, bringing the rest of us rapidly from the garden. She had dropped the letter to the floor in her shock and I grabbed it as I ran upstairs to retrieve the scrapbook. Blaire had left her phone on the floor by the bed, dropped in her haste to leave the house filled with deceitful friends. Lifting the phone I began a text from Blaire….

***

11.30 pm

'I don't understand what happened – why did she suddenly run out like that?' Emma said, shaking her head. Kirsten sat beside her, looking at the floor. I watched to see if she would speak of the letter. Even if she did, the letter was gone. I would deny having given her anything and Emma would put it down to the escalating paranoia.

'She dropped this on the way,' I said, holding out the phone. The screen showed a text which had been written but not yet sent.

'I'll be there as soon as I can shake them off! God, what a night. I'd forgotten just how provincial they all are…….'

Charlotte sadly turned the phone off.

Eddie let himself in the door and looked at us all in the living room.

'What's going on? I had to explain myself to get into my own house. The police are taping around the house. Where's Ava?'

'You'd better sit down Eddie,' I said, 'Ava is at the police station with Sam. There's been a terrible accident.'

***

Sunday

We're in all the headlines today. Top story of the day! The others are all too upset to talk to the press so I have taken the lead explaining that we, her friends, had gathered around to help her in her time of need, but that she had treated us with disdain and contempt. It appears that she had been trying to call Emma for weeks, without leaving her name, resulting in Emma's girlfriend Kirsten having a nervous breakdown. She had derided the home of her old friend, calling it 'provincial', and had flatly refused to offer any help to the refuge when asked that evening. In fact, it was just after that conversation that she fled out of the house in anger, leading to the accident. How the public perception can change in less than a week. Blaire changed from a victim to a monster between Monday and Sunday – because this world is ugly, full of selfishness and misery. Scrape the veneer and you'll see that I'm right.

THE MAN AND THE FINANCIER

It had taken only five seconds for him to decide to do it. After all, he had made something of a profession of righting what he perceived as the wrongs in the world. Somebody had to do it. The world had become too tolerant, blurring what is right and wrong; nowadays, this society that invokes us to accept that *our* truth may not be our neighbour's truth; nothing is black and white but only shades of grey. But he could not accept this philosophy, because that would mean accepting that Julie's death had been the result of a series of unfortunate circumstances, and not the fault of the driver of the bus which had veered off the road and mown her down. Nor the fault of the young man who caused the driver to lose control as he demanded the day's takings to be swept into a paper bag, holding a gun to the driver's head, in order to support his young family. Wrong was wrong, and justice needed to be served, no matter the consequences. Julie's death was now twenty years ago and he failed to see the irony of his chosen life. Increasingly fuelled by substances, his impulsive behaviour was now verging on reckless.

The early morning sun beat down heavily, making sweat patches on his back beneath the rucksack which contained the tools of his trade. The queues had not yet begun to build outside Casa Mila, one of Gaudi's most iconic works of architecture. Squinting into the sun, he could make out a few of the famous chimneys on the roof against the cerulean blue cloudless sky. Buying his ticket, he was helpfully informed by the member of staff that he could choose to see the roof first before making his way back down through the building if he wished. That was exactly his intention. Before the crowds arrived, he planned to find himself a spot on the roof where he could watch people as they stepped out into the glare of the sun; a place where he could hide amongst the shadows until his prey arrived. He didn't care how long he had to wait – he was prepared to sit it out. He had been reliably informed that the financier of the rising global pharmaceutical company would visit Casa Mila today. The same financier that had funded the development of a drug that was being sold at an unjustified cost to the poorer countries in the world, making a profit from the hardship and pain of others. He deserved to die.

"Have a nice day," he said to the pleasant Spanish lady, who watched him head for the stairs.

Reaching the roof, he stepped out into the glaring sun. He was immediately transported to another world. The roof rose and fell like it was being swept along on the waves of the sea. Incredible structures surrounded him, all different and all drawing his hand forward to touch the cool surface of the perfectly carved stone. He was fascinated by one chimney, which was like a section of an army, each wearing helmets and overlooking the city. They appeared identical until closer inspection revealed that each one had individual characteristics in shape and form. Contrasting against the perfect blue sky, the stone seemed to change in colour, ranging from tones of sepia to pale lemon. Another chimney rose like a huge, immovable flower, circular holes cut with precision, creating an opportunity for light to travel through, as well as settle on, the shape.

The Man walked up and down the stairs, along the curved walkways of the roof, momentarily distracted from his mission by the beauty surrounding him. The chimneys were positioned around the outer rim. In the centre of the roof were two huge openings, one smaller, circular and the other more a rounded rectangle – the courtyard was eight stories below, a dizzying, sheer drop. Taking up position, he watched as people began to gather on the roof. As there was only one way up and another down, it was easy for him to study each person as they emerged from the door.

Gasps of delight could be heard as people first took in the scene before them. Cameras were whipped out and countless photographs taken, people posing before the chimneys and along the rooftop, taking in the scenes of Barcelona. A family with three young children appeared, squeals of delight followed by racing up and down the stairs, covering the perimeter of the roof in minutes. Older folk picked their way less certainly, pausing to rest and admire the chimneys. Young lovers posed for photographs, standing with backs to the wall, taking selfies. Looking uncertainly at the hawkish man, nose slightly bent in the centre, features and limbs all sharp edges and carrying a rucksack on his back, a pretty blonde girl approached The Man with a camera held out.

"Would you mind taking a photograph of us, please?"

Taken aback, The Man swung his bag around a little, accepting the camera. Taking no time to frame the picture, he pointed it at them, clicked and returned the camera with a scowl. The girl moved on with her boyfriend, looking at the photo and glancing over her shoulder with discontent.

The sun was getting hotter and he drank the last of his water which was, by now, no longer thirst-quenching and refreshing, but tepid and unsatisfactory. Cursing his lack of foresight to bring more fluid, The Man looked at the people accumulating on the roof. He had not anticipated so many to be allowed up here at one time. People were queueing to climb the stairs and approach the chimneys now, and he was feeling too conspicuous. The sun was relentless, scorching his exposed arms, the back of his neck. His head was beginning to ache and he was becoming weary in the merciless heat.

The crowds might help him to quietly slip alongside his target, slide his silenced revolver into his ribs and lower him to the ground, he thought. In fact, because each person made their way around the whole edge of the roof, visiting all the sculptures, if he sat it out, his victim would at some point present himself nicely to him of his own accord. He jumped as a scream pierced the air, followed by the giggle of a teenage girl who had been alarmed by her boyfriend suddenly appearing from inside a chimney. As the sun reached its highest, black shadows appeared on the structures wherever there had been a sharp edge cut into the surface of the stone. It was difficult for him to find shelter now and he was sweltering In full sun.

A group of teenage girls were standing in front of the 'flower' chimney, one blocking the lower holes in the stone.

"OMG, it looks like a 'shocked face' emoji, look!"

Laughter ensued from the girls as they each in turn had a photograph taken and mobile phones were passed one to another. As The Man looked at the sculpture behind them, he had the impression of the Edvard Munch painting, "The scream". Perhaps it was because he had been studying Expressionist art when Julie had been killed, but he felt connected to this painting somehow. The agony of the human condition – his agony, his life overshadowed by the loss of his baby sister. The two carved upper holes represented the expressionless eyes and the centre hole the screaming mouth. As he looked at the chimney he could almost hear the scream and sat transfixed.

"I guess what you see when you look at these carvings will be dictated by age, by life experience and by the mood being felt at the time." Someone sagely remarked as they passed him.

The Man was beginning to feel claustrophobic. He wanted to get off this roof, out of this sun, away from all these people with their insignificant, shallow lives. Every shriek from some idiotic teenage girl had his nerves jangling. Every tentative step taken by an aged person, body rotting before his face, enraged him with its pointlessness. Julie was not allowed the opportunity for life – how dare they take more than their fair share. Young lovers irritated him with their nonsense and dreams of a happy future together. Happiness was a lie; it was a deception of the highest kind.

He shook the sweat from his eyes and his lank hair from his face. He twitched his right shoulder up and rolled it back, touching the fabric of his rucksack and the concealed revolver within it. His head was now throbbing and the conditions on the roof were wearying him. He pulled his wet t-shirt from his back and tried to refocus on the entrance door to the roof. Where was he, this rich and scheming financier of poisonous hope?

Man watched a girl of about nine emerge into the sun. She wore denim shorts and a ruffled pink cotton top. Her trainers were sky blue with a shocking pink sole and laces. Her head was delicate and fragile, with two long plaits sitting on her shoulders and he immediately felt protective lest any threat come to her. She reminded him of Julie. Long, skinny legs like Bambi, looking barely strong enough to hold her up. Her freckled face beamed when she saw the chimneys. She did a little dance of pleasure on the spot and he remembered Julie's response to new experiences being the same. His shoulder moved up and rolled back as he watched the girl, transfixed.

"Come on, Dad" she shouted behind her, "It's amazing!"

A man of his late forties emerged into the sunshine and The Man drew himself up. He adjusted his rucksack and stared, recognising the father from his photograph. The Financier stood catching his breath for a moment and taking in the scene. His daughter skipped from one foot to the other in excitement.

"Isn't it amazing, Dad?"

"It is, it's fantastic." He smiled, indulgently.

"Come on", the girl ran ahead, excited.

The Man watched. They were obviously close. The Financier held his daughter's hand as they admired the structures.

The girl produced a pencil and drawing pad and began to sketch the shapes of the chimneys, and the Financier did not hurry her but stood looking out over Barcelona. For a moment, a procession of schoolchildren obscured The Man's view and he had to stand to keep them in his sight. His lips were sticking to his gums and he ran his tongue between them, shaking sweat from his eyes. He brought his rucksack to the front of his body and slowly began to open the drawstring.

The girl had moved on to the next chimney and was chattering to her father as she drew.

"He was so clever, Gaudi, wasn't he Dad? To think of all this!"

"Yes, if you have a talent, it's important to share it with the world."

"I think I might have a talent in drawing, don't you think Dad?"

The Financier stooped to look at his daughter's sketch. "Yes, I think you do, sweetheart. Just like your Mum."

"Well, you have talent too Dad, don't worry. Your talent is helping to save people."

The Man's shoulder hitched and his pupils widened as he

caught this snippet of conversation. He fought down the nausea that threatened to draw attention to him. His heart began to beat more quickly and he wiped his sweaty palms on his trousers.

The pair moved towards him, unaware of his intention to separate them forever. The Man was incensed. What sort of hogwash had the Financier been whispering into the ear of this young innocent? She had no idea of the monster that she had as her father. What kind of life could she look forward to, fed lies by her father, and once he had been removed from the scene, these lies would be merely reinforced by the mother. The girl had no chance. She would lose her innocence. She may even end up with blood on her own hands. He had to protect her from the poison that would ultimately destroy her. Had they already injected her with their virus, both metaphorical and real? Was she already dying, her young mind corrupted by their scandalous claims, her body ravaged by the toxins they injected into her.

His thoughts were jumbled, he couldn't see properly because of the sweat in his eyes. He was overheated. And dehydrated. The sun blazed above him. He punched himself on the side of his head and some people passing him looked towards him nervously.

What should he do? He was drawing attention to himself. What if those people raised the alarm? The girl would be doomed to live a life of contagion, of poison. He had to do something to protect her, to get her away from harm.

Bolting forward like an animal, instincts at their height with the adrenalin coursing through his body, he sprang forward and grabbed the girl in his arms.

"It's ok, Julie," he whispered, "I've got you."

He leapt over the barrier and into the opening to the courtyard eight stories below the girl held towards his chest. Screams pierced the air as people rushed to the barrier and the sound of the Financier's voice echoed from the chimneys, "Noooooooo."

The Man held the girl tight, resisting all temptation to flail his arms as he hurtled towards the floor in his misguided attempt to rescue her from her destiny. She looked at him with terror until their bodies hit the floor. As the witnesses looked down they saw two circles of blood begin to form around the crushed skulls, mirroring the openings in the roof above, one smaller than the other, one a circle and one a rounded rectangle. As those in the courtyard cautiously approached the bodies, they took in the scene before them. The broken bodies of a little girl aged about nine, beside a man of about thirty-five; a rucksack had slipped from his shoulder and the contents were strewn over the cobbled ground – a revolver, a knife with a serrated blade of about 6 inches, two empty water bottles and an old photograph, worse for wear, showing the smiling faces of a teenage boy with a pretty, freckle-faced girl, arms around each other and sharing a joke. It was a picture of love, wholesome, untainted, untested.

UNCERTAIN STEPS

12th July 2020

His voice is mellow and smooth, the words dripping from his mouth like melted chocolate from a fondue. Polly had always loved chocolate – perhaps a little too much to look at the curve of her hips in her new pleated skirt! She makes a vow to herself to slice up that melon that's been decorating the kitchen worktop for the last few days while she had decided to forego the nutritious fruit in favour of the fatty but glorious slab of Dairy Milk. She unconsciously smooths the fabric over her hips and hitches her rain mac onto her other arm to relieve the sensation of the weather-resistant material making her skin sweat. She silently berates herself for dressing so inappropriately. Why hadn't she worn something more comfortable? Even as she asks herself that question she knows the answer. She had been desperate to make a good impression on this, her first date in more than twenty years. Desperate – that made her sound so needy!

Joseph halts at the gate, holding out his hand to steady her as she steps around another deep, muddy puddle in her completely inadequate nude court shoes. She smiles at him, embarrassed by her need of support from this man about whom she knows so little.

She has avoided dating agencies, despite living alone since her last relationship became intolerable. For a number of years, she had enjoyed the freedom that singleness brought. "Who needs a man?" she would laughingly say to her friends and colleagues as she danced until the early hours - no need for any apologies for lateness, or to tiptoe around a sleeping partner when preparing for bed. She had determined to 'live life to the max', and she did, until the novelty of having nobody to make apologies to stretched into endless days of solitude and loneliness. She had shared her home with a friend for some time and enjoyed the companionship, but it wasn't the same. The irritations of living with another person without the pleasurable 'making up' that comes with a physical relationship could be testing.

A few friends had suggested some blind dates, but the thought of any awkward early conversations with a stranger being witnessed or assessed by friends was excruciating, so she had politely declined, declaring herself to be "Fine, honestly, I'm fine." Then, a few weeks ago, after finishing a bottle of wine on her own while watching some rubbish TV that she wasn't even interested in, Polly had found herself flicking through the picture gallery of "Foxy and Fifty", set up exclusively for those still young enough to be looking for something more than 'companionship', but who are prepared to admit that they are no longer in the full flush of youth. Before she could change her mind, her courage fuelled by the alcohol in her system, she had entered her details:

Name: Polly Shaw

Age: 51

Description: (*This she had taken a little poetic license with*) Five foot 4 inches (*she was actually five foot one and half*), brunette (*greatly enhanced of late by some clever hairdressing!*) with a bubbly personality (*mostly true, except when feeling a little maudlin after drinking too much wine and feeling sorry for herself!*). Always worked in the hospitality industry, so good with people and able to put them at their ease (*no need for exaggeration on this bit!*)

Looking for........: Someone who is sociable, fun, and able to relax. Honesty is important to them and a good sense of humour too.

Choosing the photograph to share had been a challenge. Completing her registration at 2 am meant that she couldn't exactly contact any friends or family for a nice image of herself, and scrolling through the photos on her phone had presented her with a series of pictures of her blurry face squeezed up next to a friend or colleague on a night out, often in dark interiors with lots of 'noise' in the background. Finally, she had found a work photograph which she thought would be suitable. It showed the smiling face of a woman wearing her ash-blonde hair in a graduated bob, which neatly framed her face. She was able to crop the picture so that her uniform was not shown.

It was not long before she had been offered several dates, but the faces that had stared back at her from the computer screen had almost caused her to withdraw from the site altogether. She knew that any man over fifty would probably carry some baggage, and most were very unlikely to have the movie star looks of Richard Gere, but some of the men had looked downright creepy, and some as if they were living under the illusion that sporting dyed dark hair, and even worse, dyed beards which looked as if they had been painted on with a paintbrush, would keep them looking as they did twenty years ago. Then she had seen Joseph Hamer looking out at her, salt and pepper hair, looking distinguished and rather sexy, just a little long so that it flopped slightly as he tilted his head. The hazel eyes that looked into the camera were saying "Is this a crazy idea? I can't quite believe I'm doing this!". Polly had smiled, sharing the joke, and wanted to know more. And so here they were, on their first date.

Polly had suggested a National Trust property, imagining a gentle stroll through the walled garden followed by a pot of tea and a thick, warmed scone with jam and cream. She had dressed in her midnight blue pleated skirt and caramel, v necked cardigan which she wore fastened to outline her still nicely shaped breasts and small waist. The court shoes had been a necessary addition to provide her with the extra two and a half inches that she had claimed on her written description of herself!

What she had not anticipated was that Joseph would arrive with his dog in tow, who had not yet had a walk today due to unforeseen circumstances. Joseph had appeared oblivious to her inappropriate attire and suggested they walk first around the grounds, before acquiring a seat in the Tea Rooms and indulging in a fat-laden treat. Their walk had begun awkwardly when Polly had teetered on her heels, going over slightly on her ankle, but Joseph had grasped her by the elbow, the smile in his eyes exactly the same as had looked out from his photograph. She had shrugged and committed herself at that moment not to complain. The decision to wear these ridiculous heels was hers and hers alone. She would just have to live with it.

As they walked, Joseph had shown just the right amount of interest in her, asking questions without probing too much into her past. They shared a love of travel and 80's pop music and they settled into an easy conversation, which led to a game of gentle one-upmanship as they tested each other's musical knowledge. Polly stopped thinking about her sore feet and relaxed, enjoying his company. The dog, a beautiful dark red greyhound called

'Wispa' – "as in the chocolate bar, she's a bit of an airhead!" – happily trotted alongside them, only occasionally venturing a little further to investigate some scent she had picked up.

"She's a rescue dog. A bit clingy mainly, but very loving. Watch out though, occasionally she gets a bit excitable and she zips past you like an express train."

As they reach the Tea Room, Polly's pace quickens towards an empty table. When Joseph goes to order she slips off her shoes under the table and wrinkles her toes, breathing a sigh of relief. Joseph returns with the tray and reaches down to pat Wispa, who is lying on the floor beside his chair. As Joseph straightens again his eyes start to dance.

"Five foot four, eh?" – he winks.

Polly grins back. Wispa lifts her head and looks first at Polly, then at Joseph, then settles her head between her paws with a deep sigh.

**

12th July 2020

Joseph Hamer had loved his wife with all his heart. They had been childhood sweethearts and he had known no other women, romantically, throughout his adult life. Her death of breast cancer had devastated him for five years. He had retreated into work, putting off returning to the home that they had shared and which was filled with so many memories. Daisy was in every room, from the luxurious drapes which hung at the windows, to the matching towels in the bathroom. She had made their house into a welcoming home to which he returned each evening with relief after long hours in the office. They would sit together and share about their day, snuggled on the sofa, and indulge in their game of re-naming work colleagues according to which movie or TV characters they most resembled, either physically or in characteristics. Daisy had been fun and he had cherished every moment together, but when cancer had struck it was with startling speed, and she had died just 5 weeks after being diagnosed. His world had changed overnight. He made excuses when invited out by friends or family, and became angry if anybody dared suggest that, after all this time, he might consider building a relationship with another woman. A couple of the women at work had done that thing of looking at him with tears in their eyes, putting a comforting hand on to his arm to express their concern, and it had infuriated him. Then, a year ago, he had found the letter that Daisy had written.

It had taken him a long time to sort through Daisy's belongings – he had found it comforting to know that although she had gone, something of her remained. He would inhale the fragrance of her clothes while he sat on the edge of the bed, remembering her. He would run his finger along the spines of the books that she read and occasionally read one of them himself, wishing that he had done this while she was alive and they could have discussed it together. Last August, he had opened one book, "Tess of the D'Urbervilles" by Thomas Hardy, remembering that Daisy had always said that it was not only a wonderfully romantic book but that it also had one of the best and strongest female characters that she knew. As he flicked through the pages, an envelope had fallen to the floor. It bore his name in Daisy's handwriting and was dated 1984, in the earlier years of their marriage. With shaking hands, he unfolded the letter and read

My darling Joseph,

I can't believe my luck to be married to you! I have loved you since the day we met and I have always felt treasured and loved by you. You are my best friend as well as my lover, and I want you to be happy forever, but we have no idea what life holds for us. You have heard me talk about this book so many times – I do hope that one day you will read it. The resilience of the human spirit comes through so wonderfully, and Tess is such a wonderful character in how she copes with the awful cards that life deals her. I hope and pray, my darling Joseph, that neither of us ever has to face the terrible challenges that she does, but if we do, let's try to be like Tess, let's try to face it head-on and survive. We are survivors, you and me. I don't ever want those beautiful, dancing hazel eyes of yours to be clouded by sadness. We have to carry on, keep taking one step after the other, and not give up. Promise me, Joseph, promise me that you will fight.

I love you so much,

Your Daisy"

Joseph had wept; he wept and then read the book, and then he wept some more. And slowly he healed and began to find small pleasures in life again. He adopted Wispa, a beautiful, dark red greyhound that had also suffered the loss of someone she loved, after the black and white greyhound rescued alongside her from their cruel owner, had died shortly afterwards. Together Joseph and Wispa recovered, learning to both give and receive love again. Then, during an idle moment a couple of weeks ago, while browsing on his laptop, an advert had caught Joseph's attention. "Foxy and Fifty" – inviting friendship and more, for those ready to meet new people in 'middle age'. "What do you think, girl?" he murmured to Wispa. She lifted her head from his lap, looked him in the eye, and groaned and he had laughed, taking a selfie on his mobile. He uploaded the photo and registered, saying to himself, "What can I lose?".

His answers to the questions had been brief:

Name: Joseph Hamer

Age: 58

Description: Fairly ordinary-looking bloke of nearly 60!

Looking for....: Some company, I suppose. Who knows?

He hadn't done any preparation and hadn't thought much would come of it. He had spent some time flicking through the pictures, playing the game that he and Daisy had played, assigning new names to people according to which TV or movie characters they reminded him of, when he had come across somebody called Polly Shaw. The game he had played with Daisy for all those years had developed in him an attentiveness to detail when assessing a face. Polly looked pretty, open, and friendly, but concealed beneath this there appeared to be some sadness. He found himself returning to the photo to look again, and now, here he was, on his first date since he was sixteen years old, with Daisy.

The first thing Joseph notices is how pretty Polly looks in her neat skirt and cardigan, and she is wearing heels! His heart sinks – poor Wispa has been cooped up on the floor of his office all morning as something had come up which had to be dealt with immediately. He hadn't the heart to lock her indoors back home and had no choice but to bring her along. He wasn't sure what would be the politically correct thing to do. Should he apologise and suggest that Polly sits on a bench while he walks Wispa? Would that make him a chauvinist, suggesting that she couldn't keep up with him because she was a woman? Would she even still be here when he gets back? Should he acknowledge her poor footwear for a walk, or would she be insulted? Does he tell her she looks nice (which she does, very) or should he stay 'non-commital' until he knows her better? He wishes he'd done a bit of research before setting off – he was so out of practice with all this. Suddenly, it seemed important to him that he got this right! He decided that he'd better say nothing.

As they walked he found that she was easy to get along with. She had said in her description on the website that she was good at making people feel relaxed, and she was. Mind you, she had also said that she was five foot 4 and she most definitely was not that! Joseph realised that he was wondering what it would feel like to kiss a small woman like this. Daisy had been tallish, at five foot 8, and rarely worn heels. He feels that Daisy would have liked Polly, with her easy conversation and hearty laughter.

There are a few occasions when Joseph catches a frown crossing Polly's face though, and he worries that she is disappointed in him in some way, but as he walks to the counter to order their drinks and scones, he sees her slip off her shoes and watches her face relax as she wrinkles up her toes. I wonder why she wore such high heels today, he thinks, and then a smile crosses his face as the answer presents itself to him. Next time, he thinks, we'll go to a swanky restaurant where she can rest those pretty feet of hers all evening.

STAY

The grassy slope offered the best view by far – a
kaleidoscope of colour, the hubbub of competing activities with
the cacophony of untrustworthy sound systems. Hungry ambition
being loosed in parents that should know better, and tears from
disappointed children who had failed to win their event or lost
their over-priced balloon to the sky. From the right came the
sound of dogs barking excitedly, straining at their leashes as they
tried to greet each other with their customary sniff, but were
restrained by owners too busy chatting to friends to think about
the instincts of their canine companions. At the end of the field, a
young baton twirler was going through her performance one
more time, shivering slightly in her electric blue leotard and bare
legs. Other majorettes practiced their flips and cartwheels on the
grass, silent in their concentration and intent on the contest
ahead. A few stood at the edge of the rope which marked out the
arena and watched their rivals, a group of girls aged 10-12,
wearing bright red, long-sleeved dresses with short skirts and a
soldier-type jacket. A long queue snaked down the middle of the
field as younger children waited in turn with their parents to have
faces painted like a tiger, a monster, or a beautiful butterfly. At
the front of the queue sat two young women with their paints and
brushes on a table, backs aching, patiently repeating the designs
on new faces, being rewarded with a smile of delight as the

youngsters saw themselves in the mirror when the masterpiece was completed. Occasionally a painter would stretch out her back which had grown stiff from leaning forward to the children. The queue was no shorter now than when they had begun and no doubt the artists would enjoy a hot bath tonight to soothe out the tensions.

Suddenly, a sense of someone sitting down on the grass, a bag swinging slightly and knocking gently against the shoulder. No exchange of glance, no greeting, just straight in.....

'How are you?'

'Fine.'

'You don't look it.'

'How would you know?'

'I know you.'

'You used to know me.'

'What's happened?'

'What hasn't happened. Where were you?'

'I'm here now. Tell me.'

'I don't know where to start.'

'Anywhere. Just dive in. You and Carl ok?'

'We're fine. No problems like that, just in every other way,' with a shrug.

'Meaning?'

'He's not well.'

'How?'

'Unwell. Mentally, I think. Work pressures, job at risk. Uncertain times. Drowning.'

'What else?'

'My work. I don't know if I'm happy anymore.'

'What's changed?'

'Everything. Not fulfilled.'

'What else?'

'The kids.'

'Lucia?'

'Lost her way. I don't know who she is anymore. Distant. Withdrawn. We've grown apart. I keep reaching out to her but she's drifting further and further away.'

'Nick?'

'What do you think?', turning to look.

'Still?'

'Never stopped.'

'But I thought…..'

'No.'

'Is he still coming to you for handouts?'

'He tries.'

'You've stopped helping?'

'We try.'

'What else?'

'Dad.'

'What about Dad?'

'He's not well.'

'How?'

'His heart. His diabetes. His smoking. His sadness.' This last was directed like an arrow straight at the heart.

'Is he getting help?'

'When I force him to. He doesn't care anymore. Says what's the point.'

The mood is broken by a group of teenage boys who charge past noisily, voices raised in excitement and anticipation as they make their way down the hill to the festivities. They can be heard goading one another with the rush of testosterone blazing through their body.

A pause to allow the boys to move on, then.....

'What else?'

'My mum.' A sidelong glance, accusing. A heavier silence.

'Where've you been? I needed you.'

'I'm sorry.'

'You're sorry?'

'Yes.'

'It's not enough.'

'It's all I have.'

'You should have more. I needed you. It's been three years. Where've you been?'

'At the bottom of a bottle.'

'I know. Are you still there.'

'No, not the bottom.'

'Why are you here?'

'I missed you.'

'I'm afraid of you.'

'Why?'

'You might let me down again.'

'I won't.'

'Don't promise what you can't give,' standing to feet angrily.

'Three hundred and sixty-six days,' spoken quietly.

'What?'

'Dry.'

'Impressive. Congratulations,' thrown out sarcastically, tone flattened, dead.

'I've never done better.'

'So, what changed?'

'I don't know. Maturity? Health scare of my own. A new man in my life.'

'So, not for us then?' Resentful.

The sound of a brass band drifting on the wind....

'I'm here now, aren't I?'

'Yes. For how long.'

'As long as you'll let me.'

'Who is he?'

'A good man. Not unlike your Dad, actually. I have a second chance.'

'Lucky you.' Spat out bitterly.

'Don't be cruel.'

'I'm sorry.' Shoulders sagging, contrite.

'Nobody's perfect, you know.'

'I know.'

'We make mistakes. We hurt people. It's usually not intentional.'

'Health scare?'

'It's gone now. I took action.'

'Maturity?' A hint of a smile.

'I got there eventually.' Holding out a hand, an olive branch.

'I kinda liked your free spirit. Hope that's not all gone.' Accepting the hand.

'Just learned to control it.'

Standing together watching the people below getting on with their lives, oblivious to the rapprochement taking place on the grassy slope.

'Can I meet him?'

'Yes, in time.'

'Not yet?'

'No.'

'Why not?'

'Where's your Dad?'

'Why?'

'I want to see him.'

'Don't hurt him again.'

'I won't. I owe him. An explanation, at least.'

'I'm scared. How will he react?'

'He'll be ok.'

He's changed. Older, more frail …'

'I've changed. Kinder, more tolerant …'

'I don't know.'

'I do ….. It'll be fine.'

'Are you back in our lives?'

'Do you want me to be?'

'I've needed you ….'

'I'm here.'

'Mum ….'

Arms wrapped around each other, a tearful embrace, words exhausted.

Below, the small children move slowly along the queue to be transformed into a butterfly, a tiger, a monster, and the older children twirl their batons while the dogs sit eagerly in the arena, responding to the voice of their 'family' to 'Stay'.

MEMORIES OF RAIN AND MOTORBIKES

She reached out her arms in front of her, allowing the cool raindrops to pool in the palms of her hands, luxuriating in its refreshing qualities. She inhaled the intoxicating smell of the wet earth and watched as the fragile flowers were pounded by the rain which was growing in strength. Her clothes became heavy as they absorbed the water, and still, she didn't move, fixed to the spot by an invisible force. Her eyes were closed as she surrendered herself to the elements then suddenly, she gasped, eyes now open, fearfully looking around her.

"No, no, no, no, no, no..." she screamed, then a blanket was thrown around her shoulders and arms held her, strong arms to keep her safe.

"Ewan", she trembled, "Thank you, Ewan. I was so scared. I thought I was going to die."

She buried her face into his strong body, sobbing and still trembling, as the young man escorted her inside. He brought her a hot cup of tea and said

"Here y'are, Granny, that'll warm you up."

She raised her head and looked at him, confused for a moment.

"Oh, it's you, Tommy! I'm sorry son, what must you think of your old granny, carrying on like this!"

"It's ok" Tommy smiled, "but I am curious! Who is Ewan, and what happened that scared you so?"

"Och, you're not interested in all that now." She said, "Ancient history."

She took some sips of her tea, looking into the flames of the fire.

"I know my granpa was Billy, not Ewan!" he teased. "Grandpa's long gone so you don't need to worry about upsetting him. And I'm old enough not to be shocked you know!" He winked at her and her heart melted as she gazed at this strong, healthy young man, who, in many ways, reminded her of Ewan.

"When I was a girl I worked in a hotel in the harbour town of Port Patrick, on the West Coast. I don't know if you've ever been there, son, but it's a bonny wee place, houses painted all colourful and cliffs dropping down to the sea. Coming from Glasgow, it was a real tonic for me, all that fresh air and open space. I'd been one of nine kiddies, you know – there wasn't a lot of space at home. Ewan was a boy I got friendly with pretty quickly. He was 24, just like you are now, and I was 21. He worked on one of the farms over in Drummore. He had a motorbike with a sidecar on it, and we would motor off into the countryside on it whenever we got a chance."

"I'd love to have seen that Granny. Did you squeeze into that sidecar with yer best frock on?" He laughed.

"No, Tommy, there wasn't much call for a best frock for me in those days."

"Well, you'd better get out of those wet things now Granny before you catch a chill."

*

"Are you ok, mum?" Janie asked. "I've just got one more shop I need to go in."

When her mum didn't answer, Janie repeated "Mum, is it ok if we go in one more shop, or do you want to sit here on this bench while I just pop in?"

"What? Och, aye, I'll just sit here for a while."

"Ok, I won't be long." Janie hesitated, uncertain if she should leave her mother. "You won't go anywhere, will you?"

"No, no, I'll stay here." She replied.

Janie wavered for a moment, then decided to hurry to the last shop as quickly as she could. She can't have been more than ten to fifteen minutes but when she approached the bench, she could not see her mum. Panic rising, she quickened her steps, looking around for any sign of her mother. The bench was empty but there was a gaggle of people watching something, some laughing, amused at what they were observing, and others looking slightly uncomfortable, but nevertheless, absorbed by the scene playing out before them. Janie rushed towards them and made her way to the front of the small crowd. Her mother was seated in the sidecar of an old, green motorbike, handbag on her knee and looking straight ahead, while a grey ponytailed man in his early sixties looked at her, helmet in hand, scratching his head and wondering how to evict this elderly lady from his motor vehicle. Horrified and embarrassed, Janie dashed towards the vehicle.

"Mum, what are you doing? How on earth did you get in there? Come on, let's get you out so this gentleman can be on his way."

She looked at the owner of the motorbike, "I'm so sorry. I can't think what's got into her. She's been a bit forgetful lately but she's never done anything like this."

The motorcyclist replied, "Don't worry about it, hen. I'm just glad you came. I was a bit stuck as to what to do, to be honest. She keeps calling me Ewan, and telling me to stop messing around and be on our way!"

Janie sighed, apologised again, and began to help her mother out of the sidecar. Her mother glanced around and asked, "What are all these people staring at?"

"You, Mother," Janie muttered, struggling to keep hold of her shopping while helping her mother to her feet. "What were you thinking of, getting in this poor man's sidecar like that?

"I don't know. It just seemed the natural thing to do. I'm sorry, love."

"And who's Ewan anyway?" Janie asked, crossly.

"Oh, someone I used to know a long time ago."

**

"You'll never guess what she did today?" Janie said to her husband and son as they ate their evening meal. "She only climbed into some bloke's sidecar on the High Street! I was mortified!"

"Ha, ha, did she?" exclaimed Tommy. "Good for her! I didn't know she had it in her to do that!"

"Never mind 'Good for her', what on earth got into her?"

"Maybe she thought it was Ewan's bike."

Janie looked at her son in amazement. "Ewan's bike? The man said she kept calling him Ewan. Who's Ewan? What do you know about him, Tommy?"

"She told me about him a month or two ago. She was standing out in the rain getting soaking wet, then started to shout "No, no, no", and when I went out to bring her in, she called me Ewan. Apparently, it was some bloke she knew when she was a girl working and living in Port Patrick."

"Port Patrick? Yes, I remember mum told me that she spent some time there when she first left home. Something happened and she was brought home again. She never said what it was, just that she was ill and needed to be looked after, but she never went back again."

"Have you made that appointment yet with her doctor, Janie?" her husband asked. "I think your mum might be ill again, now."

"Yes, I'm taking her next week."

**

It's so quiet that she can hear the sound of the birds' wings cutting through the air like blades. Beautiful gannets soar high above the water, circling, looking for their prey. When they swoop down into their dive, the speed is incredible and they enter the water like an arrow released from a bow, with barely a splash. She can see shags resting on the rocks to her right, all facing the same direction, protecting themselves from the wind. A fulmar glides through the sky above her, riding on the thermals effortlessly. She looks down at her ankle – her foot is no longer pointing forward, but is now sitting almost at a right angle to her leg. The pain is excruciating, so she tries to take her mind off it and watch the seabirds perform their awesome acrobatics. From her position, she can't see up to the top of the cliffs, and she can't hear any human voices either. She is trying to support herself on the shallow shelf by clutching onto a rocky protrusion, but she knows it won't take much for her to continue her fall down into the sea. She imagines the shock of the cold water to her body, if she's still conscious and avoids the sharp rocks projecting from the cliff edge below her.

How quickly things can change, she thinks. Just a short while ago she was enjoying the strong breeze above, looking out over the sea to Northern Ireland and the Isle of Man. Visiting the Mull of Galloway had been Ewan's idea. He was a bit of a bird enthusiast and had been teaching her ever since they had met. He waxed lyrical about the incredible birdlife at this most southerly point of Scotland. She hadn't taken much persuasion and they had made their way on his motorbike along the winding, single-track roads, climbing higher and higher. The white painted lighthouse stood in the centre of the promontory but they headed towards the cliff edges to admire the sea birds. As they made their way they saw meadow pipets and swallows in their tens, they spotted stonechats with their splendid orange breasts and wheatears with their striking black and white tail stripe. Gannets, shags, and fulmars were plentiful, and then a Roe Deer had sped past them, its red coat beautiful in the sunshine. She had followed the deer in excitement and, being a city girl with a very limited experience of the dangers of the countryside, had not noticed the 'Danger' sign, lost her footing, and hurtled over the cliff edge. "Ewan!" she had screamed as she dropped, and had landed with a crash, ankle first, onto this ledge. She had no idea how long she had clung to this shelf now, but it felt like a long time. The weather was beginning to change and she could see a huge dark, grey cloud making its way across the water towards her, throwing down rain like arrows from the gods. When that rain hit her, not only would it lower her body temperature and possibly cause hypothermia, but it would make the rock face slippery and she was not sure that her grip would hold.

"No, no, no, no, no," she said, firstly under her breath but rising to a scream as her fear took hold. What should she do? Her ankle throbbed with pain and she knew that climbing was impossible. Her hands were becoming numb and her grip was weakening. She strained her ears for the sound of Ewan's voice.

"No, no, no, no, no………"

"Mum. Mum, you're ok. You're ok, Mum" Janie said, holding her mum's hand. Her mum was shaking with fear, gripping her as if her life depended on it.

A little girl eating ice cream on a nearby bench stared, and some teenagers passing by with candy floss glanced over their shoulder, curious at the wailing emanating from the old lady.

"I don't think I can hold on much longer. The rain's coming. The rain ……. What can I do?" Her words come out breathlessly. "What's Ewan doing? Is he getting help? How long has it been?"

Janie embraces her mother, rocking her gently and soothing her, ignoring the prying glances of people passing by.

They have been here many times now over the past twelve months. The doctor had said that memories may be triggered by any number of things and it may not be possible to protect her from them. Particularly traumatic experiences may be relived time and time again until the dementia progressed to a point where the experience was completely erased. The family were gradually gathering the fragments of memories and beginning to construct a picture of what she had gone through, though they may never know the complete story. It seems that she had a friend/boyfriend called Ewan who had a motorbike with a sidecar. They would go out together in this and at some point, an accident had occurred – whether this was a road accident or some other form of accident was unclear, but she appeared to have been separated from him and feared for her life. Obviously, she had survived, but, as she had never mentioned Ewan until she had become plagued by these memories, they had no idea whether he had survived or not. Was he killed in the accident? Was this the accident that brought her back to Glasgow? Why did she never return to Port Patrick? Perhaps these details would emerge in time, but the family are beginning to understand the triggers for the attacks. Rain, especially heavy rain; the sight and sound of sea birds and the sight of an old motorbike and sidecar. It seems that until these fearful memories are erased, they must be ready to console, to reassure, and soothe her tortured mind as they wonder what happened all those years ago.

SAVING GRACE

Her heavily made up face was as smooth as porcelain, and just as brittle. Her cheekbones were accentuated to make her face appear more angular, her eyes emphasised by black kohl and lips painted deep red, outlines etched with the precision of a surgeon's scalpel. It was a mask projecting an image to the world to distract from the reality within, to protect a vulnerability. She was required to perpetuate the impression that she had cultivated for so long – that of a strong and loving marriage, two people in harmony in both their work and their relationship, for the two were so intricately bound that any divergence in one aspect of their partnership would inevitably bring the whole crashing down.

Grace assessed herself in the large mirror and smoothed the vermillion silk skirt of her floor-length dress. The slender figure of her youth remained not because of good genes but through hard work and dedication to their 'brand', the enterprise that they had begun together not long after leaving university, with all the zeal and confidence that comes with youthful ignorance. In those days Ian Barrett had been an exciting new designer, full of ideas and creativity; he was able to capture the zeitgeist and interpret it in the use of colour and fabric, shape and volume. His designs had quickly made an impression on the catwalks all over the world and were easily able to be replicated by the high street brands. Grace, with her tall, slender figure, was a perfect mannequin for Ian's designs, and together they inserted themselves in the higher echelons of the fashion world. To begin with, their relationship was purely professional. They had become friendly as fellow students on the Fashion Design course, working together on several projects. They found that they each stimulated the creativity of the other and it was so easy to be around each other that it was only natural that they should continue to work together after they had graduated. Grace, though brimming with ideas, tended to be a little taciturn in public, becoming tongue-tied and unable to organise her thoughts, so Ian had stepped forward into the promotion of their products and Grace had gradually evolved into model and muse. Over time they had become lovers, many of their best designs conceived and drawn whilst they lay in bed, post-coital. Ian had made it pretty clear early on that it would be only designs that should be conceived between them and Grace had sadly set aside any aspirations for motherhood.

In truth, throughout their partnership, the designs had been composed collectively. Ian's flair for capturing the spirit of the times being restrained slightly by Grace's understanding of what could be translated for the High Street, and what women would actually wear away from the catwalk. Being 'the front-man', it was Ian that drew all the attention, and there developed an assumption that the designs were all his alone, Grace being the beautiful goddess that inspired his talent. Ian had felt that any attempt at clarification would merely muddy the waters, and after all, the most important thing was that their designs were appreciated and made their impression on the catwalks. Whenever Grace had raised the subject, he would simply say "But darling, I am just doing this to keep you safe. You know how much you hate answering questions from reporters. You just keep on wearing our designs on the red carpets and your face will continue to be in every newspaper and glossy magazine in the world. There is no-one better than you to wear our creations, because you know them, you feel them as they are meant to be. It's you that sells our designs Babe, not me." Grace, being by nature tractable and hating any disunity in their relationship, would smile and try not to allow herself to feel downtrodden or resentful.

Grace makes her way downstairs, the soft fabric of her dress sliding off each step like molten lava. The two upper staircases meet from left and right into a central sweep into the large hallway, where Grace turns left towards the drawing-room, where she knows that she will find Ian. On entering she sighs as she notes that he already has a large whisky in his hand.

Seeing her unspoken rebuke, Ian retorts "It just whets my

appetite, that's all. You know what I'm like at these ceremonies. I'm all on edge, wondering if we've won, so I can't eat when they serve the food, then you get annoyed with me because I've drunk too much on an empty stomach. I'm doing it for you really, Babe."

Grace walks to the cabinet, replacing the lid on the whisky bottle. She knows where this conversation will go. Being from a relatively humble background, Ian will become maudlin about how he has never really fit in with all the upper crust that we will find ourselves sitting beside around the table this evening. They haven't had to work as hard as we have, it's all just been handed to them on a plate. She has noticed over the last few years that, as Ian's creativity has begun to wane, his confidence has plunged. She cannot recollect which came first, the drinking or the decline in productivity, but she does know that she has been carrying him now for at least five years. He hasn't contributed a single idea in the last two years, and the latest collection was wholly designed by Grace. She had worked night and day, even sitting alongside the seamstresses at a sewing machine bringing her designs to life. She was happy with the end products and felt that she was finally ready to step out of the shadows and be recognised for the work she had done. Ian had barely noticed that Grace had taken care of all the promotion of the collection and had steered the necessary press conferences and meetings away from him. The dates of the various ceremonies in the Awards seasons were usually ingrained upon his mind and he was aware as these approached but the recent months running up to them were, to him, a blur of alcohol-induced fog.

Grace walks to Ian and brushes the shoulders of his charcoal and air-force blue checked jacket. She hesitates when she spots some dirty marks on his black roll neck jumper – ordinarily, she would ensure that he looked immaculate for these evenings, after all, he was the spokesman of their brand – but perhaps tonight would be when the truth came out. Could she do this? Should she do this? Looking at this man before her, who had robbed her of the chance of a family; who had taken all the glory for their designs for twenty years and never once, not a single time, acknowledged her input, except as a glorified clothes horse to display his wares. He had used her, diminished her confidence, stolen her ideas, and sold them as his own, and now he was in danger of destroying everything through his self-pitying, drunken rants. It dawned on her that he had always been a weak man. A stronger man would have had the courage to make it plain to the world that they were a partnership of designers. She looked into his watery, fogged eyes and felt little sympathy.

"Come on", she said. "It's time."

They stepped in from the rain into the large Hall and spent some time drinking champagne as they milled with other designers before heading to their table. By now Ian had lost any reservations that he may have had and was loudly commenting on people as they made their way to the table.

"Look at the spare tyres on that one!"

"There's nothing original about that little creation – seen that a million times."

"See the state of that posture? She as bendy as a tired old carrot".

Grace ignored his remarks. She had heard them all before and was tired of his embarrassing monologues. She had done with trying to defend or protect him.

Ian picked up the booklet featuring the nominees, rifling through it to find his name. His eyes rested on a paragraph detailing the collection that Grace had designed. The short piece made it very clear that Grace had been responsible for all aspects of the work.

Slamming his drink onto the table, Ian exclaimed "What's going on here? Stupid idiots have messed up the programme!"

Heads turned to look at him as he gestured wildly, now on his feet but unsteady. Grace watched impassively, refusing to intervene. Around the room large screens flickered into life, each bearing the name and brand of the nominees. A murmur could be heard around the table as people noticed the re-modelled logo, which made no reference to Ian. Ian stared at it for a moment then brought his gaze to meet Grace's. "You? What...what's going on?" he said.

Grace did not reply and Ian slumped into his chair. The game was over, and so was the deception. Oh, she would not abandon him – they had been through too much together, but it would now be on her terms. She was stepping up and taking charge of her own destiny. It was her time.

YELLOW

To Valerie and Graham,

You have never really known me, have you? You have been too wrapped up in your sorrow to notice me. I understand why you have been so sad, of course I do. I miss her too. I always looked up to her – being ten years my senior she was a goddess to me. I trusted every word she said and copied everything she did. I remember her too, though I don't think that has ever occurred to you as you have been so consumed by your own pain. You had two daughters, and in losing one, you went on to forget the other.

Every achievement in my life has been received by you as a memory of Alison, so instead of celebrating with me when I learnt to ride my bike, did well at school or performed in a school concert, I would see the tears in your eyes as the memory played behind them of a different girl who had done these things before me. I did not want to cause you pain and so I stepped into the shadows where the spotlight would not fall. And in a house which is shrouded in shadow, I was seen less and less by both of you, as you tiptoed around each other's grief. I never made friends at school because I could not have invited them to my home. You would not be able to bear their joy and childish abandonment, their noise and irreverence in a house which has become a shrine to Alison. And I would not have been able to bear the inevitable comparisons of me to Alison when my friends saw all the photographs hung on every wall – her so pretty with her soft, chestnut hair falling to her shoulders, face alive with laughter and confidence, compared to my mousy long plait and my long fringe hiding my glum features. Who would want to be friends with that anyway?

And so, I have crept around the house through my whole childhood, invisible to you both at home, and invisible to the people at school, blending into the background, surviving each day before returning to my room to sit alone with a book or daydreaming at my bedroom window.

There have been moments of happiness – watching video clips on my phone of a cat chasing a light, or a baby giggling and its parents laughing with it with a love so deep that it can't be described by words. Did we ever do that? I can't remember us laughing together, can you? The unwritten rule is that we can't be happy, because that would mean that we had forgotten Alison.

As I have lived in this dark and solitary world I have begun to see the world in colours – it helps me to navigate my way and make sense of my life. Red is the colour of anger, but also of embarrassment, or something shameful and taboo like my monthly period. This colour has loomed large in my inner life, like a fire being constantly kindled in my heart as more and more fuel has kept it alive. Brown is the colour of love – earthy, essential for growth, the deeper and denser the colour, the better the depth of love. I have witnessed that colour surrounding Alison but I have only experienced for myself a dry and dusty beige. Green is hope, new birth, fresh growth - I haven't seen much green for a very long time. Yellow is the colour of happiness - pure and warm, a colour that can envelope somebody in its rays. Occasionally, for a moment or two, I can almost reach orange, but never for long, and never at home. Mostly, my life is blue/grey, nothing striking, nothing to stand out and make you notice, just plodding along in muted colours.

But, like a kaleidoscope, the colours of our lives can change in a second - it takes only one colour fragment to completely alter the picture from blue to yellow, and the fragment which has done this to me is called Sandy.

Last week I reached my limit. I was so weighed down by the black that I saw no hope. I have lived in the shadow of Alison for most of my life, and with each year that has passed, I have waited for you to remember me, to show me that you love me, that you are proud of me, that you value me. But I don't feel any nearer to that than when I was a six-year-old girl sitting alone and unnoticed in a roomful of adults weeping and comforting you in your grief. When I walked out of the house last week I had not formulated any plan, but I knew that something had to change. I am not Alison, and can never replace her. I can never be good enough. I made my way to the lake and, while I was gazing at the water, it began to rain. Not gentle raindrops but heavy pelts of rain hammering against my skin. I felt as if the sky was shedding the tears that I was no longer capable of. I allowed them to drench me as if locked in a trance, not caring about sodden clothes or wet hair. Suddenly, I realised that an umbrella was being held over me. I turned and saw that a girl my age, wearing crazy clothes, had sat down beside me and was silently shielding us both from the rain. As I looked at her she smiled, a smile that asked no questions and made no judgement, just exuded warmth and understanding. We sat silently for what seemed like ages and the rain gradually began to ease.

"Where did you come from?" I asked.

"I've been watching you for a while. You seemed so sad, just staring at the water like that. And when you didn't even move when it started to rain, I figured you might need a friend."

I started to cry quietly. How could I explain? Who could possibly understand? I didn't know where to begin.

"I'm Sandy", she said, "and I live just there." She pointed to a house just opposite the lake.

We didn't talk much more that day, just sat together and watched the water. I went back the next day and sat in the same place and before long Sandy had joined me. She never probed; she just let me be but made sure I wasn't alone. Eventually, I began to tell her. I told her that I was invisible, I told her how much I missed Alison, I told her how much I missed you. I told her how sad you are, and how sad I was. I said that I had no worth, there was no point in me being around. She listened, then she hugged me and let me cry some more. Yesterday she persuaded me to go to her house for something to eat and to meet her mum and I surprised myself when I agreed. It's just Sandy and her mum - her dad left when she was young. The house is bright and cheerful, full of things they have found beachcombing over the years. The windows were open and the breeze coming off the lake blew the curtains, making them billow out into the room. The curtains are burnt orange and the chairs mismatched with clashing colours. Looking out of the windows I could see the brilliant blue sky and the colourful sailing boats on the water. We laughed together as Sandy told me about the scrapes she gets into and her mum occasionally made remarks from the kitchen as she prepared some snacks. I almost made yellow! And they have invited me to stay for a while, to add some colour to my life.

Please understand. I love you very much, but I'm going to stay with Sandy for now, because Sandy is yellow – unadulterated, glorious yellow. She can never be in the shadows – she is joy, she is laughter, noise and sparkle. She is a riot of colour with her red hair and freckled face, her bright clothes with wild patterns that fight for your attention! Her golden yellow has brought me hope, has brought some light into the darkness and I am praying that her yellow will turn my blue into green shoots of hope for the future, for my future.

It was her idea that I write to you to explain, to introduce myself to you – my name is Ginny, I am sixteen years old and I'm your daughter, the one that is still here.

xxx

TRUTH

She reclined on the small bed in the living room, leaning on her right side, as if in a Renoir painting. Her grey hair was worn long and loose, but unbrushed, and her large heavy breasts overhung the edge of the mattress. She was naked, save the thin blanket which covered from just below her navel. Three fans were positioned around the bed, circulating the stale air and directing a constant breeze onto her body. She was without embarrassment or reserve and conducted our conversation unabashed. I, on the other hand, felt ill at ease and awkward, unsure whether, in my efforts to look unfazed by her nakedness, I was being too direct in my gaze. In truth, I was overwhelmed by conflicting feelings of awe and inadequacy. This woman before me had achieved everything I was striving for — success in her field, respect from colleagues across the world, travel, love, even a confidence in her body that felt no need for cover or adornment.

***

"Lisa, I want you to get to the bookstore in town and get the story of their 10,000th book sold. Leave now, and we're looking for 500 words." Sam, the Chief Editor, shouted across the noisy office.

"Ok, Chief."

I picked up my bag and slung it over my shoulder, collecting my notepad off the top of the desk. Five hundred words on a book shop winner, great! Hardly going to win the Nobel prize for that piece of reporting am I, I thought. Well, I suppose even Bob Woodward and Carl Bernstein had to start somewhere before they uncovered the Watergate scandal, leading to the resignation of President Nixon. And, to be honest, I do feel passionate about supporting local bookshops. I worry that pretty soon we will be buying everything online and they will be a thing of the past.

I've always loved wandering around a book store. It appeals to all of my senses, from the smell of the freshly printed paper and hot coffee in the modern stores to the fusty, airless smells within those treasure troves which sell innumerable older books, sometimes first editions, spread across bookshelves and piles, with no apparent classification or ordering system to help the prospective buyer. It was in having to dig through these mounds of books that you could sometimes discover a gem that you hadn't even known existed. Only a few weeks ago I had been on my knees lifting books from a crate in the darkest corner of the shop when I picked out a slightly battered hardbacked book fronted by a striking photograph of three African boy soldiers. The boys were aged, I guess, between about 12 and 15. Each had a weapon slung over one shoulder, soft peaked hats, and held a cigarette in their hand. Two were engaged in a conversation and the third, the eldest, looked directly into the camera lens. They had the brazen, confident look of soldiers twice their age. The book was full of newspaper reports covering the Angolan War of Independence in the mid-seventies, and the images were extraordinary. I had felt compelled to buy the book and have been reading it hungrily ever since.

This book shop, though, was more modern – the type that invites customers to sit down on a comfortable armchair and peruse the books on offer. A welcome sanctuary amidst the scurrying crowds of people pushing their way along the street. On entering the shop, I was greeted with a smile and an unhurried welcome, and was able to absorb the sense of the place without being pushed towards a sale.

"Let me know if you need any help." The young man said, returning to the book that he was reading whilst drinking his tea.

I spent a few minutes wandering among the shelves and observing my fellow browsers – an elderly gentleman was standing in the 'Military' section, turning the pages of a large hardbacked book that seemed to be celebrating military medals. A young father was seated on the floor with his young daughter and they were laughing together at the book he was reading to her. A teenage girl was browsing the 'Art' section, running her hands along the spines of the books as she went, evidently searching for a very specific book to help with her studies. A lady in her fifties was looking for inspiration amongst the 'Top 50' paperbacks. Dotted around the shelves were 'Staff recommendations', where staff had helpfully written a short review on the books that they had read. These were the things I loved in local bookshops – suggestions of reading that would probably never have occurred to you, but sometimes introduced you to a whole new world you have never navigated before. Summoning all my willpower to remind myself that I was not there as a potential customer, but rather a reporter from the local newspaper, I introduced myself to the young man at the counter.

The shop had been struggling of late, the numbers of customers falling as more and more people were buying books either online or in the charity shops. They had tried a number of different initiatives to advertise the shop, the latest being an offer of a small 'Book hamper' to their 10,000th customer in their 40-year history in the town. The plan had been to invite the winner to the shop, invite the local press, and maybe do a Q&A with them, asking what books meant to them and for a list of ten recommendations which could form a display in the shop. However, this had backfired somewhat, as the winner was apparently bed-bound and could not visit the shop, usually ordering her books to be delivered. Her list of 'Recommendations' had also proved to be of a very narrow genre, all on the subject of

African wars in the late 20th century – not necessarily a subject that would inspire the customers in the shop that day, except, perhaps the elderly gentleman. I was given the contact details of the winner and arranged to visit her. The name sounded vaguely familiar to me but I was unable to place it.

I arrived at the property and struggled to open the gate, resulting in threatening barks emanating from inside the house. Nervously, I walked to the door, hoping that somebody else would be present who could perhaps put the dog in another room while I carried out my interview. When I knocked on the door a voice instructed me to enter and I hesitantly stepped into the hallway. A large black dog bounded up to me, still barking, but quickly responded to the commands of its mistress, leading the way into the living room. She called him over 'for a kiss' and he lovingly walked to the side of the bed, licking the fingers of her hand as she lay on the bed. I had been completely unprepared for the sight that greeted me, but she was friendly and invited me to sit. Apologising for being unable to offer me a hot drink, she proceeded to question me about myself. How long had I been a journalist? Was this my first post? What sort of articles had I written so far? What was my passion? Did I have a plan for my career? Who did I admire? She was a talented interrogator and quickly unearthed my passions, my insecurities, even my heroes in the world of journalism. In answering her questions, I discovered thoughts I had never actually voiced before or even been conscious of. I stopped seeing her nakedness and instead became aware of a sharp mind and her attentive interest in me and my ambition. It was with some difficulty that I eventually redirected the conversation towards the reason for my visit. She was patient and open, answering my questions and including added details that would add interest to my piece.

It was hard not to notice the piles of books around the room. I could not see any fiction on display. The books were all factual and the majority seemed to be on the subject of war. Suddenly the pieces fell together and I remembered where I had seen the name before – Rachel Wright, a journalist featured in the book I had recently acquired in the old bookshop. Rachel Wright – who had reported on the widespread discrimination against native African soldiers within the Portuguese army during the Angolan War of Independence, prejudice evident even as they fought against the insurgent groups across the Angolan countryside. She had travelled with the army into the heart of the conflict, putting her own life in danger from both factions, while she reported the truth of what was happening. When I tell her that I have read some of her reports and admired her work in getting the truth out to the world, she exhaled mournfully.

"Truth. What is truth? Even Pontius Pilate didn't know the

answer to his own question. Some say truth is relative – it depends on your point of view. It changes according to your particular perspective. But for a journalist, truth is fact. It demands clarity. There is no room for sentiment, for judgement or opinion – just facts, pure and simple. And eventually, I had to make a choice."

I thought back to the articles I have read, articles in which Rachel had highlighted the treatment of the soldiers, reporting on their harrowing experiences and the injustices she had witnessed. Was she suggesting that she had sold out in some way? Not been authentic?

"A choice?" I prompt.

"In the end, we are all undone by love." Rachel lays her head on the pillow, eyes looking at images that only she can see. "Chilala Cardosa. That was his name. He was a young man, idealistic, honourable, honest. And so very handsome." She smiled.

"We would chat around the fire in the evenings. He had been assigned to look out for me, keep the irritating Englishwoman 'out of harm's way', preferably out of the way of anything really." She laughed sardonically. "He was attentive and kind, and though quiet in the company of the other soldiers, he would open up if we were alone and tell me of his family back home in Portugal. I grew to look forward to our chats and found myself falling in love with him. He would ask about what I would be putting in my reports and I discussed my observations with him. Then, one day, I woke to the sound of shouting and gunshots and discovered that Chilala had defected to the People's Army of the Liberation of Angola. He wasn't alone, a group of the African soldiers had left together and it was a political nightmare for the Portuguese. As a journalist, I was expected to report the facts. That would include detailing the treachery of this group of men, who had turned their backs on their country - treason, defection, deception. Any report I wrote could not be biased, despite what I had seen. It would mean betraying Chilala and our evening conversations. Those private, precious moments that I could not risk sullying by the interpretation and judgement of those who would not understand. That was the end of my career as a journalist. I chose love."

We sit quietly for a while, both deep in our thoughts.

"Did you ever see him again, Rachel"

She shook her head sadly. "No. I have tried to locate him over the years. I have scoured every book and every report I can find, trying to find something, anything. To know what happened to him. Did he survive the war? Did he return to his family in Portugal? I've found nothing."

I pulled the tattered old book from my bag, "Fallout –
Stories in the wake of human conflict in Angola". The faces of the
smoking boys looking out. I handed the book to Rachel.

"Have you seen this one? I found it a few weeks ago at the
back of an old shop."

Rachel looked at the book, defeated, then reached
forward, her eyes becoming more animated.

She began to turn the pages. The book was a compilation
of reports from many international journalists over the period
1960 to 2000, including Rachel's, but it also brought together
hundreds of photographs taken from war photographers too.

I sat for some time watching her turning the pages,
carefully inspecting each photograph, searching for Chilala. She
paused on an image of a young boy being taught how to load a
rifle. He was being taught by a tall man caught in semi profile as
he guided the child's hand. The man was looking down so his eyes
could not be seen in the image, but as I raised my eyes to look at
Rachel, I could see that she had begun to weep quietly. Below the
photograph was a caption which read, "Two days after this
picture was taken, this camp of the Insurrectionists was attacked
and taken by the Portuguese army, leaving no survivors." The dog,
sensing that his mistress needed his comfort, walked to the side
of the bed and began to lick her hands. Rachel did not speak and I

quietly slipped away, leaving her with the book in her hands.

Three days later, carrying a copy of the newspaper under my arm, I entered the gate of Rachel's property, surprised to find the house quiet and no sound of the dog responding to the potential threat of a stranger. I had knocked a couple of times when a neighbour opened the door.

"She's gone love. Took her away yesterday"

"Gone where?"

"Not sure to be honest with you. She went off in an ambulance. Sitting up in a wheelchair wrapped in a blanket. She didn't look ill or nothing. Just staring ahead. Didn't say anything when I shouted to her."

I've spent the last couple of weeks searching the hospitals, the old folk's homes and the obituaries, and I can't find her anywhere. She has disappeared as swiftly as her Chilala did all those years ago. I believe her house has been cleared and her books donated to the local bookshop, where she never did receive her Book Hamper. The kindly young man, slightly bemused by this donation, allowed me to sift through the books and I recognised many of them, but was unable to find one particular book, " Fallout – Stories in the wake of human conflict in Angola". It had disappeared as decisively as Rachel had, and I was glad.

THE LONGEST DAY

"The rhythms and routines of your day to day existence, the way you organise your time, the way you spend your money, the people you spend time with – all of these things expose the very heart of us……."

Jo was only half listening to the speaker now. She was imagining a different life in the sunshine on the other side of the world. She could feel Edward's arms around her waist, his breath on the back of her neck, tickling slightly and making her shudder with delight. But then this blissful image was eradicated by the sudden, prickling sense of foreboding that she had been unable to shake off since the move to Australia had been mooted.

"Your life is a by-product, a consequence, a repercussion of the decisions that you make, day by day, hour by hour, minute by minute….."

'Oh my,' thought Jo, 'this is all getting a bit heavy. I could do without this just now.'

Squeezing along the row of chairs, apologising to the slightly rattled women as she knocked them with her oversized handbag, Jo made her way to the exit.

Would this day never end? She had spent the last twenty-four hours changing direction like the tide, first allowing her thoughts to rush her towards the soft, sandy beach of Western Australia, filled with promise and enthusiasm, only to then feel herself withdrawing, aware of the uncertainty and niggling suspicion that was beginning to mount. Edward expected an answer tomorrow. She was fairly sure that whatever she decided, he would be going anyway. His mind was made – the job of his dreams was awaiting him, with almost double his present salary to boot. And who could blame him?

Jo knew that friends had thought she'd rushed into this relationship far too soon, the classic rebound from her failed marriage, the actions of a woman robbed of her security and self-respect.

'You're moving in together?!' Polly had exclaimed when Jo shared her plans with her, somewhat hesitantly, only eight weeks after beginning a relationship with Edward. 'You don't even know the guy yet!'

'Yes, I do,' Jo had replied defensively, though she had to admit she felt a lot less sure than she would have liked. 'He makes me feel good, and safe, and cherished.'

'Humph!' Polly snorted, unconvinced. 'It's only a year since you and Phil split up. Why make such an important decision so soon? Give yourself some time.'

'It just feels right,' said Jo, 'Please be happy for me.'

Jo pressed Polly's fingers between her own and felt the pressure returned by her friend.

'I am happy for you, honestly.'

In truth, Jo was beginning to concede that she was losing herself a little since she'd met Edward. He had taken on a protective role, rather unnecessarily in Polly's opinion, and Jo's strength and survival skills had been blunted. Her normal feisty, independent streak was subdued as she snuggled into his shelter, cocooned and safe but beginning to feel just a little bit constricted and limited. For the last ten months Edward had become the decision maker, choosing how they spent their time, and, increasingly, their money. She was seeing less and less of Polly and missed her. How would she cope on the other side of the world away from her friend?

Edward had taken it for granted that Jo would move to Western Australia with him and tempers had flared last night when he realised that Jo had misgivings. She'd asked for time alone to think about it and he had ruthlessly laid down a deadline of 36 hours. They would meet tomorrow morning and she would give him her decision. All day she had wrestled with herself, changing her mind, noting down pros and cons, trying to be rational but was no closer to her decision now than when she'd woken.

Acknowledging that this was something she needed to resolve for herself, she resisted the temptation to seek advice from friends or family, though her final decision would, of course, have consequences for them too. This evening's 'Lifestyle conference' had been in her diary for weeks and she'd hoped it would help her to see things more clearly.

'Not so far!' she thought as she left the building. 'Perhaps a walk home will help to clear my head.'

Pulling on her padded coat against the bitter wind, she turned towards the town centre, keeping close to the buildings.

***

'One more sleep and then it's your big day, sweetheart!'

'Yippee! Then I'll be four!' said Jasmine, giving a little twirl in her Cinderella dress and gaudy, pink, plastic-bejewelled crown.

'Grandma, Grandma!'

'Yes, darling?'

'Actually, I've got something really excited to tell you!'

'Have you? What's that?'

'It's really, really, really excited, Grandma!'

'What is it?'

'Today I saw guinea pigs and they were eating flowers and leaves!'

'Was that at nursery? That sounds wonderful. Which one was your favourite?'

Jasmine gave this some thought, then answered 'The golden one.'

Her grandmother laughed and swept Jasmine up in her arms for a hug.

Jasmine had awakened her mum at 5am this morning, believing her birthday to have arrived. She had little understanding yet of the words tomorrow and yesterday, and lived her whole life in 'today' – probably something the adults could learn from her! After she'd woken, she'd climbed into the double bed for a cuddle and her mummy could feel the gathered skirt and soft velvet of her new dress, bought especially for her birthday celebrations. Several hair clips had been placed randomly about her head and felt cool to her mummy's lips as she dropped kisses onto the little girl's hair.

She was allowed to wear her new dress for an hour or so before reluctantly taking it off again and going to nursery. Jasmine was disappointed that it still wasn't her birthday. She knew it was going to be soon because everybody kept saying so, but it *still* wasn't here!

'Have a good day, darling.' Mummy had called as she left Jasmine at nursery. The nursery nurse led Jasmine to her coat peg which had a picture of a flower but it wasn't actually the right colour. This flower was pink, but a real Jasmine flower was pale yellow. Jasmine didn't really mind though because pink was her favourite colour, and sometimes purple and sometimes blue. Mummy said she had been named after the flower Jasmine because it smelled so beautiful, not because of how it looked. Anyway, sometimes Jasmine pretended that she had borrowed her name from Princess Jasmine from Aladdin and it wasn't a flower at all.

All day at nursery she had told people that it was going to be her birthday and that she would be four. When they asked her what she was going to get for her birthday, she knew all the answers to say – 'A Frozen II Elsa dress, two cupcake princesses and a new crown'. That had made all the grown-ups smile and she liked making them smile.

Then Grandma had come because Mummy went out – Yippee! That meant lots of fun and treats, although Grandma had needed a little bit of help with the treats part this time.

It was *ages* ago since Grandma kissed her goodnight – surely it must be her birthday now! Jasmine climbed down from her bed and moved over to her wardrobe. Opening the door, she saw her new dress. She knew that it was a navy blue and white polka dot dress that felt really soft, even though she couldn't quite see it properly because it hadn't got completely light yet. She took her Paw Patrol pyjamas off and put the dress on, then pulled some new knickers from the drawer. She selected her favourite headband, put it on her head, pushed back her loose hair from her face and made her way to her Mummy's bedroom.

***

June settled herself into the sofa and switched on the television. She could do with a bit of distraction to be honest, to stop her mind from going into overdrive.

'It's not as if you've ever been exactly a beauty!' she scolded herself.

She couldn't resist her hand reaching to her face again to touch the skin just left of her nostril. She could feel the raised area, about the size of a pea. How long had it been there? She couldn't really be precise when the doctor had asked. She was a practical woman who'd been too busy raising her child and helping her to navigate a confusing and frightening world to be bothered with being concerned about her looks. It was only when she began to experience the itchiness that any alarm bells had gone off, and when the same itchiness came in the centre of her spine and the back of her neck, she had thought it prudent to seek advice. Her doctor had seemed concerned and immediately sent her for further urgent investigations. Of course, she hadn't told anybody about them. No point in alarming people until you know what you're dealing with – that was her motto.

Years ago, people used to draw moles on their faces, didn't they, as a sign of beauty? Curious that the thing women thought beautiful has turned out to be so deadly.

'Get a grip,' June muttered to herself. 'Deadly! You're getting a bit ahead of yourself there.'

She opened the TV magazine to see if there was anything worth watching. Nothing probably. What she didn't want just now was a hospital drama or factual programme about skin conditions, cancer, or some sort of modern Victorian freak show! Just a nice gentle programme to take her mind off things.

'Urgent' the Specialist had said yesterday. 'Need to act quickly.' 'Need to know what we're dealing with.' 'There might be some options, if we're quick enough.' Well, tomorrow she would find out. Was it only yesterday that she had been asked to strip in that fluorescent-lit room and had every inch of her body examined by that nice young woman who was wearing the rather alarming head torch and magnifier thing? June had felt so exposed. She couldn't remember the last time anybody had seen her naked body. The doctor had been very solemn after June had replaced her clothes.

It seems her body was covered with the darned things. The Specialist had counted 4 on her back, two on the back of her neck, a couple on her buttocks, one on the back of her arm and the beginnings of one on her forehead, in addition to the prize specimen in the centre of her face. She had an appointment first thing tomorrow morning and she didn't know how she would sleep tonight. The day had felt twice as long as a normal day, so how long will those dark hours seem, staring up at the ceiling, with her mind whirring.

At least she'd had a little distraction this evening. Spending time with her granddaughter was always such a joy. She could be so funny sometimes. June placed the magazine onto her lap as she replayed in her mind the amusing scene following teatime, when Jasmine had said,

'Grandma, I'm hungry.'

June remembered how they'd enjoyed a picnic last week, when she had prepared a fresh fruit salad of pineapple, satsuma, grapes and strawberries. Jasmine had devoured much of the fruit, enjoying the variety of colours and textures.

'Shall I make you another one of the fruit salads, like we had on our picnic?' June asked, conspiratorially.

'Well, yeee-ss,' Jasmine had answered, unconvincingly,' but I'd like something *un*-healthy with it.'

June had laughed, pulled her granddaughter into a tight hug, and searched the cupboards for something suitably 'naughty' to add to the fruit.

Sighing, June thought about her daughter. She could see so much of her in Jasmine – bright, quick to learn, independent. She'd been devastated when her marriage had disintegrated and had withdrawn into herself. At first Edward had seemed heaven-sent – a kind and gentle man who loved Jo and made her happy, but over the months June could see that he was too protective of her. He treated her as if she was fragile, insubstantial almost, whereas June had raised Jo to be robust. She needed to be to survive.

What would the future hold for her small family? Would she be there for much longer to support Jo? Tomorrow she may be wiser and she could begin to plan, but until then, she had these endless hours to pass.

Hearing a noise, she turned to face the door. Jasmine was standing, blinking in the bright light, wearing her pretty, polka dot dress and a headband which failed to control the strands of hair partially covering her sweet face.

'Is it my birthday yet, Grandma?' she asked, sleepily, 'Am I four?'

June put out her arms to her beautiful granddaughter, and

gathered her onto her lap, planting a kiss on her warm cheek.

'Not yet, sweetheart. It's still night-time'.

'Still?' she asked, disappointed, sucking the back of her hand.

The front door opened and June heard the tell-tale sound of the probing cane being placed in the umbrella stand in the hall. Jo appeared at the door, one hand slightly outstretched, feeling her way along the furniture.

'Hi love,' June said, 'How was your evening?'

'Confusing,' said Jo. 'How was yours?'

'All ok here,' June replied, 'although I have a little girl on my lap who is desperate for her birthday to come!'

As Jo took her seat, Jasmine climbed from her grandma's lap to her mother.

'Mummy? When will I be four?'

'Soon darling, very soon.'

Jo brought her nose to her daughter's head and inhaled the smell of strawberry bubble bath. She slid her hand expertly over her daughter's body and noted the soft fabric of the special birthday dress and the mis-aligned headband, ineffectual atop the mass of hair.

The three sat in companionable silence for a moment, lost in their own thoughts. The day was coming to an end and tomorrow was a momentous day for each of them, their lives forever changed.

'I love you, Mummy,' Jasmine said sleepily. 'And I love Grandma too.'

In that moment Jo made her decision, as she sat with the two most important people in her life. There was a potency in the love that they shared, a strength that she had lost sight of but things seemed clearer now.

ABOUT THE AUTHOR

Sally Nicol was born and raised in Manchester, UK. She has spent her whole working life as an Occupational Therapist and draws much of her inspiration for characters from the interesting people she has met through her work and in the parishes of her husband, who is a Church of England minister. She has two much loved grown children and two treasured grandchildren.

Printed in Great Britain
by Amazon